Stories from the Twisted Tree

Stories from the Twisted Tree

Alternative Entertainments Arts Group

Stories from the Twisted Tree

Published by Alternative Entertainments Arts Group, 2006
ISBN 0-9547235-3-8 978-0-9547235-3-8

Edited by Caroline Barry and Neil Richardson

Cover photo by Caroline Barry

Book design and layout by Lir Mac Cárthaigh

Contents

Brief Editorial

Stories from the Twisted Tree is the third publication of work by aspiring young writers, this time from the Midlands. Over 2006 these young writers would meet every week, one group in Kilbeggan Library the other group in The Heritage Centre in Tullamore. All of them worked hard, developing characters and stories and finding that most elusive and precious of all things, their own voice. It was a pleasure working with both groups. I want to congratulate the contributors to *Stories from the Twisted Tree* and wish each and every one of them success for the future. I would especially like to thank Alternative Entertainments for having the vision to invest in such a long-term project. I would also like to thank the Westmeath Arts Officer, Catherine Kelly, the Offaly Arts Officer, Sinead O'Reilly, the Arts Council and the Department of Community, Rural and Gaelteacht Affairs. Without these partnerships the project would not have happened. Thank you.

Caroline Barry

Luke

Margaret Walsh
14 yrs, Kilbeggan Writing Group

Chapter 1

On the shores of the Island a little green boat floated serenely on the salt water. There was an eerie cold in the air. It was dark, too dark to see. But he could still feel them in his presence. He knelt in a clearing in the centre of the island, the words flowing from his mouth. Words nobody could hear. In his hand he held a staff. Time was with him. In the distance the drums roared. His voice grew louder and louder until he was shouting, screaming. "*Sed libera nos a malo.*" Then everything went silent. Not even the whispers of the ocean could be heard. His eyes sprang open revealing the intensity of the inferno that burned within. He rose and ran from where he was sitting. In his wake he left a gold ring.

* * *

The grandfather clock in Matthew's office struck three. It's tone was dull and monotonous, suggesting that sometime, somewhere it had served a purpose, but now the clock just stood there bored with time, waiting for something to happen. Matthew Barnas observed this with interest as he stood by the window looking at his empire. Within the dust and dirt that encompassed the quarry he could make out three men sitting on an old Hammersmith cart, they looked deep in conversation about something or other. Elsewhere he could see the draught horses that hauled the granite trotting wearily under their heavy loads driven by the workers from the local town. He knew the workers hated him. He didn't really care. From his window he could see the local town protected by hills on all sides. There was still snow on the peaks but winter was over and with the spring came a new year. In the far distance he could see the ocean like a stepping-stone to heaven rise from between the two hills that formed the Minuet valley. The local town of Foxtople was populated by the poor and uneducated, and the poor and uneducated were useful to Mr. Barnas. Turning to sit at the desk Matthew heaved a sigh and buried his head in his hands. Why did this happen? It wasn't meant to be like this, or was it?

At that moment there was a loud, rasping noise at the door and Jonathon Muskly stepped into the large room. Matthew had jumped up from his seat and stepped gracefully into his business-like mode. For a moment there was silence only interrupted by the heavy breathing of Jonathon. He had had a head cold for so long he could no longer hear himself snuffle. Impatiently Matthew spoke.

"Yes Jonathon, do you have a message for me?"

Matthew's voice sounded like the distant cry of rolling thunder. Jonathon looked down at the floor trying to avoid maintaining eye contact with his boss. I hate you he thought, stroking the carpet with his right foot and then hated Matthew even more for having such nice carpets.

Jonathan could be described as mousy. He was small and at the age of 30 had almost developed whiskers. Due to many years of patience and a lack of interest in life he had climbed his way up until he had acquired the grand title of personal assistant to Mr. M. Barnas, the quarry owner. How awfully fortunate!

"Well, I'm sorry to trouble you with this sir but errrrm. A majority of the workers are threatening a strike on Tuesday morning. The first day of the Suoivusev Project."

Matthew threw his eyes to heaven.

"Just give them another raise in wages. I don't care as long as they are working. You know how important an order like that is to the quarry. Use your brains boy that's what I pay you for."

Jonathon could see the veins in Matthew's forehead highlighted to a deep purple and he felt the blood rush to his ears.

"Yes Mr. Barnas, Sir." spat Jonathon through gritted teeth. When Jonathon left the room he kicked the coat stand by the door in a fury, but his rage quickly disappeared when the stand nearly fell over dispersing coats and hats on the floor.

"Sorry, sorry, sorry" he whispered before questioning himself on why the hell he was apologising to a stupid brass ornament.

In his office Matthew had other things on his mind. Accountancy books were spread out over the huge mahogany desk. Matthew just couldn't understand. The numbers didn't add up. There was a deficit of almost 100 guineas in the last year. Taking a small wooden box from a drawer close to hand he opened the lid and took out an imperial cigar. Bending his head down to the flame of his Italian lighter he lit the cigar, sat back in his chair and exhaled, letting clouds of smoke crowd the air in little swirls. He was in way over his head and Matthew knew it. He closed his eyes and thought of Claire. Since last autumn there had been a deep void between them. She just seemed to slip further and further away from him.

Chapter Two

Claire lay on the cold tiles, still and silent. She watched sullenly as a single drop of urine fell from the latrine. Her skin felt brittle from the stream of tears that had fallen from her hazel eyes. The sunlight flooded the room masking her vision. She felt so weak. A sudden wave of nausea overcame her. She lifted her head over the porcelain washbasin and threw up. Her mane of auburn hair fell in ripples across her back. The palms of her hands were damp with sweat and her eyelids were barely open. Slowly Claire grasped at the wall in an attempt to lift her weight. Her slender hand swept the gentle green pattern on the wall and fell finally onto her lace drawers. She dragged herself up onto the bench in the corner of the room and sat with her knees closed up to her chest. Gazing languidly out of the sash window she thought of Matthew, sitting in his office overlooking the quarry. How could she tell him? They had decided to put it off for later years. Not anymore. She couldn't ignore this.

Looking at the towel stand she saw the iron that Mathew had bought from her at the Foxtople market all those years ago. She remembered so vividly that first day when they had met. Claire had been selling tin cans and bits of rubbish at a stall at the very corner of the market. The market was drawing to a close and she was gathering all the bits of metal together. It was cold and wet and Claire amused herself by pressing the mud in between her boots very slowly, making shapes along the stall end while she waited for someone to collect her.

Suddenly a tall, dark man turned the corner. Not seeing Claire he ran straight into her, knocking all the items from her grasp and into the mud, completely defacing her artwork on the earth. He bent down to help her pick up her things. He smelt of menthol. Refusing his help Claire fumbled on the ground trying to retrieve her bits but in vain as she kept slipping, completely undoing any attempt she made at looking angry. He had laughed at her.

She turned to a deep tone of fuchsia. She felt so foolish standing there beneath his gaze.

"Are you going to stand there all day smiling at me or are you going to buy something from me?" She asked abruptly.

Calmly Matthew said, "I'll buy it all."

He then put a hand into his pocket and pulled out a gold coin. Claire took it from him in amazement, her skin brushing against his as she did. She quickly stepped back. Her hand uncoiled away from his. She turned the coin over and over. Never in her life had she had in her possession such an amount of money. Picking her jaw up from the ground she stood straight and looked the man in the eye. Claire had strong features a large nose and deep brown eyes that were well set in her face, but it was her mouth that was her best feature. It made her look as if she was always smiling, a big smile that showed her pearly, white teeth. She wasn't smiling now though.

"Is that all you have she stuttered?

The man just smiled in response, gathered the scraps of tin together and walked away.

Claire stared after him, what a rude man, she thought. She turned and went on her way kicking the ground angrily as she walked. Her hand firmly wrapped around the sovereign coin in her pocket.

What a rude man.

But the next day he was there again and the day after that and all the days after that. A faint smile crossed her face as she recalled how often Matthew would ask her to dine with him, or to accompany him to a dance. She always refused him. But after a time she admitted to herself that she had fallen for him that first day when he had ran into her. He made her feel all the things she should feel.

She had to tell him tonight. She hoped he would listen. Just as Claire was about to rise to dress herself, one of the maids, named Martha, sauntered into the room with a pile of fresh towels, singing the latest tune she had heard with the highest notes. When she saw Claire, Martha jumped with surprise. Claire noticed the look of embarrassment that crossed the serving woman's face.

"O sorry m'lady. I'll leave you be." Martha excused herself. But just as she was walking out the door she turned and in a fleeting moment Claire recognised a look of pity in the maid's eyes. Who did Martha think she was? Claire hated pity.

Martha had never seen her mistress in such a state before. Claire's face was tear stained and she had not dressed yet and it was nearly noon. It was obvious the mistress had a lot on her mind. There were rumours around the house and heaven forbid this was not the time for, well, another presence in the house. But everyone knew the business of the quarry. It was in trouble. Martha shook her head sadly before commencing with a verse from her favourite song.

Chapter 3

The house at great rock endured the rest of the day in silence until Matthew returned home that evening. It was late and outside the elements prepared for a storm. Matthew closed the great oak doors behind him and stood still in front of the stairs, his hand still on the door. He could feel her watching him. He wanted so deeply to hold her, to tell her it was okay, wipe the tears from her cheeks, but instead he removed his coat and hat and placed them carefully on the coat stand. He then retired to the parlour where he poured himself a large whiskey and sunk deep into his chair. Upstairs on the landing Claire sat watching from a dark corner.

Will he ever love me again after this? She thought solemnly.

In her hands she clasped a piece of needlework. It was a Madonna, an unusual piece, she knew. Mother and child together in a perfect world. It was only a picture. Struggling to complete the image she stabbed at the canvas, guiding the needle in and out in swift, angry stitches. Carelessly she continued until she caught her index finger on the point of the needle. She started to bleed. A single drop of blood fell and landed on the woman's face in the picture. She was crying, tears of blood and Claire knew how the woman felt. She knew those tears came from within and as she sat there in her fragile state Claire could feel those tears well up inside of her. She could feel those tears build in her stomach and climb furtively upwards and wrap themselves around her throat, tighter and tighter. They stayed there and refused to go away. Claire threw the cloth on the carpet and moved down the stairs in long, rapid paces repeating a mantra in her head. Everything will be okay; you will have your happy ending. She could feel herself getting hot. *We* believe in happy endings don't *We*? Everything will be okay. Just tell him. He will understand.

Out of the pitch black, suddenly a light could be seen coming closer and closer.

O God, please don't let this be it. Not yet I can't die now.

Claire froze on the stairs. Her hand grasped the banister so tightly that the blood ran from her finger and her knuckles became white like the snow on the moor. Then the light disappeared and there was silence: just silence. Outside there were footsteps followed by voices. There was someone outside. She wasn't going to die after all. She could hear an eloquent voice, it sounded so familiar, she felt at home. Then she heard it more clearly. A man saying, "he's my brother. He'll be in ecstasies when he knows I'm here."

"Hastel!" exclaimed Claire. The hairs on the back of her neck standing on end. She began to run, down the stairs, through the corridors, the kitchen, the pantry, the back door. Out of the house and away.

Matthew was soon awoken from his own, sad world by a knock on the door. It was the metallic ring of silver on wood. A sound Matthew had always dreaded ever since childhood. But he rose and greeted his brother with surprising hospitality.

"And what have I done to deserve your presence here tonight, brother?" Matthew asked earnestly. Hastel smiled broadly.

"May I come in?"

Matthew stepped aside and gestured for the tall man to enter. As he passed Matthew noticed the little manservant cowering behind Hastel. The manservant was nothing more than an acc-essory, an ingratiating dwarf-like figure employed to satisfying an ostentatious mans pride. Matthew smiled sweetly at the dwarf, provoking a nervous smile, which made the manservant look like he was trying to remove his last meal from his teeth.

Matthew turned only to find Hastel sitting in his chair sipping politely at a large brandy. "Make yourself at home" offered Matthew icily.

"So, tell me how have you been keeping?" enquired Hastel intently.

"Well" replied Matthew topping up his drink noticeably.

"And Claire, how is Claire?" asked Hastel stretching his neck, eyes sparkling, laughing internally like a cat would when offered food.

Matthew snapped suddenly, shocking himself. "Hastel are you going to sit there all night talking pleasantries or are you going to tell my why you really came?"

Undeterred Hastel carried on. "Well I'm sure you have heard of my ventures abroad and how my success has been limited?" purred Hastel.

"Yes" smiled Matthew, his fingers running up and down the glass impatiently.

"So I have left them behind me. But recently a man came to me and offered me an opportunity I cannot refuse. He offered me the chance to go in with him on an automobile business."

Matthew laughed abruptly "Let me guess you want me to give you a push start in this venture with the help of the profits from Daddy's quarry."

Hastel posed theatrically on the edge of his seat. " May you stead me?" he asked.

Matthew started to laugh, at first quietly until the noise grew louder and sicklier. It was a twisted and painful laugh. At first Hastel tried to join in, but realising there was nothing to laugh at he stopped. Matthew started to shake.

"The quarry is facing bankruptcy," he murmured.

In the meantime Claire stumbled on the stable yard. The cold of the night consumed her and she rushed hurriedly over the cobbles. She struggled to grasp for air. Her dress was torn, she felt like she was watching someone invade her stables. She wanted to scream and shout at that young girl.

Why are you doing this to yourself? GO HOME.

Instead she kept running. Finally she stopped still. She couldn't see anymore, her eyes were so cloudy and the night was so cold, so angry…

Somewhere far away Claire could hear hooves. She could feel warm breath on her cheeks. Slowly her vision came back to her. She blinked. A horse, no not just any horse, a beautiful horse, black as the night with a flowing mane and tail. She blinked again. It all made sense now. Determinedly she pulled herself up. Finding an old barrel Claire mounted her little steed. Only when the fourteen hand pony moved did Claire remember how utterly terrified she was of horses. Only when the pony gathered speed did Claire open her mouth to scream but nothing came out. No sound. All empty. Her mind flooded, all she could think was of Hastel.

How could I, she asked over and over. How could I have let this happen?

She remembered that night. It was clear and fresh. The air held a promise of new beginnings. She had waited for Matthew and it soon got dark. He never returned that night, just like so many other nights before. She remembered being so angry. So lonely. So vulnerable. Then Hastel called. He seemed to be her redemption, her revenge. He held her so close. Next morning he wasn't there. She remembered his hands and her eyes filled with tears. It hadn't been her fault, had it? Claire had erased it from her memory, until tonight. But now she had no doubt; the infant she was carrying was his.

The horse stopped moving. Claire gasped realising where she was. It was just as she remembered it, the little house in the forest, the sanctuary of her youth. She dismounted slowly and crept to the door. Gazing stealthily around her Claire saw the Belladonna growing in the little garden at the back of house.

Xanthe must help me.

She curled her fingers and knocked once, twice, three times.

Dirty Harry

Rory O'Keeffe
17 yrs, Tullamore Writing Group

BILL WAVED ME in; setting his steaming coffee down on an already coffee-ringed newspaper that was casually thrown across his desk. I could smell it from my place at the door. It could have woken someone from a coma.

"Take a seat James," he said, following his own instruction. I sat down slightly hesitantly in the chair in front of his desk. He ran a hand through his hair as if testing for baldness.

"Tell me Jimmy. I can call you Jimmy right? Are you a religious man?" He fixed me in his gaze, suddenly serious.

"Uh, no sir I'm not." That had me off balance; it's not exactly the first question you expect when called to your new boss' office.

He waved his hand dismissivly in the air. "Yes, yes, who is these days, eh? But I mean, do you consider yourself part of an organised religion?"

"Yes. My parents were Catholic sir and that's how I've been brought up."

"Good, good... So you believe in the Catholic God then, correct?"

"I guess so sir..." I trailed off. It's hard to qualify an answer when you aren't sure of the subtext.

He poked a stubby finger at my chest.

"Well forget it, Jim. From now on you have no God save for the details, you hear me? You worship at the church of evidence, hearsay and good old-fashioned rumour, understand? If you want, your priests are anyone who knows something you don't. People fucking up, disasters, tragedies – *they* are your daily bread. And let me tell you something, Jimmy, what you do or do not know, what you can and can't back up, they're the things that will make or break you in this business. Unless you got the drive, you're at nothing. Just get up and walk right out of the building. Do you get what I'm saying to you?"

I nodded dumbly. "Yes sir. I'm not walking away." I mean, what else are you supposed to say to a guy who obviously takes two scoops of crazy in his morning coffee?

"Okay son, then go out there and write me a gospel!" He pushed me through the door and shut it behind me. I heard the clicking as he pulled the string and dropped the Venetian blinds. Slightly more intense than you expect on your first day of work experience. I must have been showing my shock, a kindly looking young woman came up to me with a commiserating expression.

She looked me in the eye for a second as if taking in my horror. "Oh no, he gave you the religion speech didn't he? That man…" She clenched her fists by her sides and made an exasperated noise, "…is impossible. Don't worry, it was nothing personal, anyone with a religion who comes in here gets it. Atheists aren't generally hired… I've seen him at work on many a new guy. He leaves the blinds open every time as if to remind the people in here that beneath that hard-looking exterior beats a harder heart. As if we could forget with these deadlines… But yeah, don't worry about him."

"I'll…uh… try not to… thanks."

This woman was very pretty; dark hair and bright green eyes, her trim body wrapped in a v-necked white blouse and dark skirt. I became aware of my face turning red. I suddenly felt very conspicuous in my striped tie, obviously borrowed from my father, as were the super shiny black shoes. I started tapping my feet nervously, rolling my weight back onto my heels, the polished footwear hitting the wood flooring with loud clacks.

She put her hand on my back and I winced slightly. "You're heading out with a traffic guard today, the boss wants you to write him a day in the job, so he hooked you up with a friend of his' son who works a speed gun on the roads. Should be fascinating stuff." she said with a roll of her sparkling eyes. "I promise I'll try and get you on something better for tomorrow, once you have that report written." She started guiding me towards the lift with the hand on my back. I hoped she couldn't feel the sweat through my shirt on this unseasonably hot day. "I'm Aoife by the way, I'll be looking after ya for the next couple of weeks, so if yus have any problems come and find me and I'll sort yus out. *He–*" She jerked her free thumb at the office in the corner, "–won't be much comfort I'm afraid."

I laughed, though I wasn't sure if I should or not, and let her show me to the lift door. She pressed the button and it opened almost straight away. "Your man'll be waiting in reception to take you to the car, so good luck out there. I gave you my number, if yus have any problems gimme a call yeah?" She had to say the last bit in a rush as the lift door closed, her voice rising to a high pitch as she inexplicably went up on her tiptoes to shout through the crack in the door. She had not, in fact, given me her number.

When the lift creaked open, the fairly sterile reception area greeted me, all white linoleum flooring and faux-leather chairs around an Ikea coffee table stacked with *Hello* magazines and newspapers. Very dentist's clinic. Sitting in one of the chairs, engrossed in the opposite wall, was a young-looking man in a blue Guarda uniform. I would have put him at around twenty-nine or so. He was opening and closing his mouth in a fishlike manner and I wasn't entirely sure whether or not to disturb him. I gave him a minute to notice me, before I cleared my throat and walked over. He stood up quickly like I had interrupted something he shouldn't have been doing.

"Sorry to keep you waiting officer, I'm James Spillaney, the work experience guy."

He looked at me with a dopey expression. "Oh not at all, 'twas grand, I entertained myself, didn't even notice the time!" He offered his hand. "I'm Officer Duggan, Steve Duggan. I'll do you a trade James; you can call me Steve if I can call you Jimmy, agreed?"

"That's fine by me, pleased to meet you," I said, grasping his hand. It was warm and had a lubricating sheen of sweat.

"Right, yeah..." He ran his hand up his face and up into his dark, sweat-dampened hair as if searching for a clue. He snapped his fingers. "Right yeah, the car. C'mon I'll take ya to it, I parked it round back on double yellows. One of the perks of the job, ya know," he said with a conspiratorial wink.

I smiled like I thought that was exciting, and followed him out the revolving door of the building. His car was indeed, parked on double yellow lines. And badly; the car's back left tyre was on the pavement, yet somehow he had manoeuvred it so that the front left tyre wasn't. I climbed into the passenger seat.

"Feckin' boiling the last week isn't it? Had to sleep naked last night my bedroom had gotten so hot. Sweat everywhere." He made a wringing motion with his hands before reaching for the ignition and I grimaced at the image. "This car's just as bad." he announced, blowing air out noisily and undoing the top button of his shirt. Fearing that this action threatened a repeat of last night's efforts to stay cool, I jumped in quickly.

"Yeah there's a hosepipe ban in England I heard. Anyway, where are we headed today Steve? You're a traffic cop right?"

"Yup, that's the one. Well normally I head out to the main road nearby, park up as out of sight as I can get and point my speed gun at passing cars. To spice things up a little I like to park in different areas of the road, maybe switch sides sometimes. I like to keep things interesting, ya know?"

"I can imagine. You ever consider accountancy Steve?" I said under my breath.

"Mm I'm sorry I didn't catch that?"

"Oh nothing. You're clear on my side," I said, looking over my shoulder at the road.

"Thanks." he said, accelerating up the street. "So, how long've you been on work experience?"

"First day today, I'll be there for two weeks."

"Oh, so, you wana be a reporter?"

"I'm not sure yet. Maybe, maybe not. I used to be undecided and now I'm not so sure!" I laughed.

He glanced at me with a puzzled expression. "You do realise that you basically just repeated yourself there, don't you?"

"Did I? My mistake..." I banged my head against the window with a dull thump.

"Did you say something Jimmy?"

This was painful. "Do you like the radio Steve?" I inquired hopefully.

"Yeah, actually. One second now..." He fumbled his way across the dashboard and pushed one of the smooth rubber buttons. Dance music began pumping out of the speakers, along with a London accent.

"Yo yo yo pee-pawl! We're bringin' dahn the 'ouse right 'ere on Blast Ninety-Free, the station that puts *you* right in I-beef-ah!" Steve started nodding his head and tapping the steering wheel.

My head hit the window for the second time.

We finally arrived at his "stakeout point" at around ten thirty. It turned out to be a small tree-lined avenue just off the main road. There was a small grassy area on my side of the car with creaky swings and a graffiti-covered slide. Apparently, Daz had indeed been here, two thousand and three. What an honour.

"This is where the magic happens Jimmy," he shouted over the pulsing beat, reaching behind me to a box on the backseat, gingerly pulling from it the plastic speed gun. He held it up reverently. "And *this* is my lady!"

"Cool." I said, with as much conviction I could muster. Truth was, I was half asleep by this stage. "Show me."

"With pleasure," he said, pointing it at a passing Ford Focus. A number flashed on the screen. "Well, there's a careful driver for you!" He grinned at me.

"How long you been doing this Steve?"

"Hmm let me see..." he looked at his hand, counting the digits.

"...whoo, I'd say about six years!"

"And you never got promoted?" I asked, incredulous.

"Oh, they offered me promotion a couple of years ago but it would have meant far more time in the office and far less time behind this baby," he patted the speed gun affectionately, "Yep, me and ol' Sheila here have had some good times." He gazed at it, eyes unfocussed. I began to feel deeply uncomfortable, like someone who had walked in on his parents at play and heard that apparently dad's clamps were just too tight.

I coughed loudly. Steve snapped out of his reverie and glanced around. "Okay," he said, stretching his neck, "Now, we wait." He settled into position with a notebook on his knee, a pen in one hand and "Sheila" in the other, his eyes fixed on the black screen on the back of the gun, with red numbers flashing up, digital alarm clock style, every passing car.

Every so often, the gun would beep, and Steve would scribble down a license plate number, shaking his head and tutting, a strange look on his face like he was sucking a lemon. The first time, I was actually impressed. "How'd you get that number so fast?" I asked.

He tapped his head with the end of his pen, smiling. "Photographic memory. My noodle remembers every number, no problem."

"Whoa, that's pretty useful, must've been great in exams. I'd kill for a photographic memory!" I exclaimed, latching on to the one interesting bit of conversation in the last two hours.

He frowned at me. "It's not all good. I have these dreams... Numbers flashing in my head over and over... license plates, speeds, phone numbers sometimes... It's... horrible." He shuddered and turned back to the screen with his shoulders hunched, ending the conversation. There was a haunted look in his eyes like you see in Vietnam war veterans reliving their experiences.

At about one o'clock, after an excruciatingly boring two and a half hours with Steve and Sheila, Steve announced that it was lunchtime. Just as we reached the main road, a car came flying along and a youth in the back seat hurled something at our windscreen. The something was a water balloon, filled with what, when oozing down the glass, looking like custard. The youths in their souped up Micra accelerated away, laughing.

"Son of a bitch!" Steve yelled, hammering the steering wheel. "Fucking bastards I'll fucking show them!" He slammed the accelerator to the floor, hitting a button that set off the siren. I was pressed back in my seat as we swerved out onto the road, just ahead of a truck. The truck's horn blasted and Steve whipped his head around to glare at it, a feverish light in his eyes I had never seen before. They were wide and wild looking beneath his furrowed brow. The hair on the back of my neck stood up, little beads of sweat popping out on my brow.

He wrenched the gearstick around in its socket as we sped up the lane, sliding across to another to avoid a Fiesta and then back onto it again as he almost touched a minivan's back bumper. He was hunched up so much on the steering wheel that his chin nearly touched it, intent on the Micra attempting to traverse the lanes to put some distance between themselves and our car.

"Uh... Officer Duggan?" I tapped his shoulder lightly. No response.

He suddenly reached across me and snapped open the glove compartment, pulling out a revolver from the midst of its handkerchief wrapping. It was sleek and polished, obviously well looked after. A bullet was visible in every compartment.

"Jesus Christ I thought you guys didn't get guns!" I pressed my self back in my seat, trying to put some distance between me and the gun he held in front of the glove compartment, just over my lap. My feet scrabbled on the Bart Simpson foot mat. They had never tapped so fast.

"We don't. It's mine." He unbuckled his seat belt. "Take the wheel Jimmy I'm going out. Get me close." He began to push his head and arms out the window, placing his foot next to the gear stick to get leverage.

"What the fuck are you doing?" I yelled, hysterical, grabbing the wheel with both hands and trying to get my leg over the gearbox to get it on the accelerator. He didn't reply, his hair whipping around in the slipstream outside the window as his shoulders went through. I could see him trying to aim at the Micra. The crazy fucker was going to fucking kill someone but what could I do? Who argues with a guy holding a gun?

I swerved to avoid rear-ending a Laguna and Steve clambered back in, thudding back down in his seat and grabbing the wheel once again, resting the gun on top of it. "Had to get back in, that's a hell of a lot harder than it looked in the movies!" He grinned crazily, his words coming out breathlessly. "Move your foot Jimmy I'm guna catch these boys if it's the last thing I do!"

"You better not make it the last thing *I* do you crazy son of a bitch!" I yelled, pulling my foot back awkwardly, my pants snagging on the gear stick for a second. He gave no sign that he'd heard me.

"I'm going to try and blow out their tyres okay? Just keep it steady I'll handle the speed." His words were barely discernible above the wind that was coming in the window and buffeting us. I snatched the wheel for the second time and it slipped around in my sweaty hands. I gripped it so tight that my hands hurt while he leaned his gun arm on his other and sat the pair of them on the window frame. "I said steady!" He roared at me before returning his head to his shoulder. "Closer, just a bit closer."

The sound of the gun, despite the wind, was deafening to me, so loud and sharp that I clamped my eyes shut and couldn't open them for a second. The ringing in my ears was so painful that my eyes were watering and I felt like I was going to cry. I think I did, I'm not sure. My eyes got blurry as I looked towards Steve. He was shaking his head and moving his lips, something about hitting the ground, but I couldn't hear him over the ringing. I looked out at the traffic and saw the blue Micra pulling in on the side of the road. Steve wrenched the wheel out of my hands and pulled the car across the outside lane and up about ten meters behind the Micra.

He jumped out of the car with his gun pointed at the other car, as one occupant, a shaven-headed youth with a conspicuous stain on the crotch and down the legs of his bright white track-suit bottoms, climbed out of it. He was crying and screaming something but I couldn't really hear him.

I leaped out of the car but I didn't know what to do. Steve looked about ready to use that thing on the guys in the car and I had no way to stop him. "Jesus Steve it was a feckin' water balloon! Are you absolutely batshit-fucking-loco?" He waved me back with his free hand.

"Get back Jimmy, get back in the car. Tell Sheila what's happening, tell her to call for backup on the radio."

"It's a speed gun you bloody head case, a fucking speed gun. It can't call for–"

"I said tell Sheila!" He bellowed, eyes still fixed on the youths, all of which were now on their knees begging for mercy, tears streaming freely from their eyes. I thought I could smell the sharp tang of urine over the car fumes.

I raced to the car and grabbed the plastic gun. I knew what I had to do to stop this. I sprinted out in front of Steve, between him and the boys. I threw the speed gun down on the dusty tarmac.

"Get out of the way Jimmy."

"I'm not going anywhere. If you don't put the gun down, I'm guna stamp *Sheila* into oblivion." My voice was shaking.

"You couldn't." he said, gravely, all friendliness gone from his voice.

"I'll do it don't worry, I-"

"No, you aren't hearing me Jimmy. You *couldn't*. My Sheila is made of reinforced plastic. It's guna take more than daddy's size tens to break her my friend. If you try, I'll take you down."

Shit, I thought. This wasn't going to plan at all. I had to think fast, my eyes darting around the scene. "Maybe *I* can't crush her," I said, picking the speed gun off the floor and steeling myself, "But I bet that traffic can!" I hurled it as far as I could, onto the other side of the road. There was a crack as a bus rolled over it.

The noise could just as easily have been from Steve's psyche. He collapsed to the floor, bawling like a baby, the revolver slipping from his grasp and clacking on the ground. "Sheila!" He cried, clawing at his face.

Several hours later I stumbled out of the Guarda station, where Aoife was waiting to pick me up and bring me back to the newspaper offices, where my ma was waiting.

"How are ya Jimmy?" She said in a concerned tone of voice. "Jay-nee, when we heard at the office..."

"I'm fine, thanks." I was too tired to get embarrassed by the pretty woman. "Were you talking to the guards? They wouldn't tell me what was going to happen."

"Yeah, I interviewed a couple. I recorded it so you can use it. It's your scoop Jimmy. I wouldn't wana take this away from ya."

I nodded. "What's guna happen to Dirty Harry?"

"You mean Officer Duggan? Off the record I was told he was headed to a psychiatric hospital out of Dublin somewhere. They say that six years on traffic duty drove him insane. He was never offered a promotion, they say they forgot about him, didn't come to the office much. The one the system forgot, you might say. Off the record, though. The Gardaí are trying to keep this quiet. It's quite an embarrassment to the force. But we'll get it out there even minus those details, I don't know how they expect to keep it quiet with so many witnesses, not to mention the lads yus chased..."

"Good luck to them." I said quietly. My eyes were killing me, my hands still shook despite the injection I had been given. "Go back to the office Aoife, take your car. If it's all the same to you, I'm taking the LUAS."

Black Angel

Eva Burke
17 yrs, Kilbeggan Writing Group

– Excerpt –

AMY DROPPED OVER the cemetery wall, landing with a soft thud. The moonlight was so bright it temporarily blinded her and caused her to stumble over a protruding rock. Landing heavily on her hands, she swore loudly, then looked around in alarm. Reminding herself that no one sane would be in a graveyard at two in the morning. She pulled herself up.

The only reason she was here was to ease her mind and quieten the voices in her head, which had haunted her since Kelly's death, two weeks previously. She recalled how shocked and horrified the community had been at the circumstances, they called it the most gruesome murder in decades. Kelly had been found alone in her house, her parents missing without explanation. She had been virtually decapitated, left on top of a wardrobe. Every mirror in the house had been broken. No one had taken the tragedy worse than Amy. Kelly had been her best friend. Her parents sent her to a psychiatrist, but it hadn't helped at all.

Since then, Amy's grief had drawn her further into herself. Her days were spent alone in her room. But nothing sheltered her from the gossip which had spread like a disease and had eventually reached her. They were saying that Kelly had been involved with a cult that practised vampirism and that her killer wasn't a random psychopath. Of course the rumours were just nonsense created by someone with nothing better to do, but it had disturbed Amy so much that she needed to face Kelly's grave for the first time. Being an impulsive person she had chosen that very moment. She didn't think her parents would mind, since the graveyard was only across the road from their house.

Now, that she was here, the whole thing seemed a bit ridiculous, but Amy didn't turn back. Reaching Kelly's grave she stopped dead. Unable to believe her eyes, she gasped in horror. Kelly's grave was marked by an enormous marble angel, at its feet lay what looked like the remains of a small animal. Its entrails were scattered across her grave. The horrific image made Amy stumble backwards. Heaving, she threw up on the grass. Her mind racing, she began to run and didn't stop until she reached home. Collapsing onto her bed, her mind finally slowed and she was able to process her thoughts. Shuddering, she pictured the scene once again. Surely, she thought, surely this must all be some kind of nightmare. Her mind in turmoil, she fell into a troubled sleep.

Waking the next morning, the whole thing seemed like just another one of those terrible nightmares that had plagued her over the past two weeks. As she lay in bed, staring at the early morning sunlight, last night seemed a million miles away. Whoever had murdered Kelly, she reminded herself, would soon be locked up where he or she belonged. Yet there seemed to be an ominous feeling in the atmosphere. It tainted the air and made the room colder. Whoever had murdred Kelly, a small voice reminded her, was still at large. The bizarre circumstances had led the police to believe that it may have been a ritualistic murder committed by someone who would kill again.

This thought caused her to shudder. Glancing out the window, she saw that it was a sunny, bright day, a sunny bright day that couldn't lift her from her misery. She hadn't been to school since the murder and her parents hadn't tried to make her. The idea of going back without Kelly was unimaginable. It had been suggested that she change schools, but talk of the murder had spread so far that there was nowhere she could and remain anonymous.

She was an object of fascination for the people who craved information. They didn't seem to realise that she was as clueless as any of them. That the murder had hit her like a bolt of lightning and she was still reeling. All the talk of cults and rituals had unsettled her, but everyone seemed caught up in the morbid details of it, not focusing on the fact that Kelly, her best friend had been murdered.

In a month or so, people would get bored and move on, occasionally remembering Kelly as just another victim of some demented psychopath. But Amy knew, somehow, that this was different. Who would want to kill Kelly? She asked herself for the millionth time. This was the question that tortured her. Kelly had been a normal teenage girl with no enemies to speak of. The search for her parents was continuing to no avail.

She absent-mindedly switched on the TV and flicked between the channels. Most of the early morning news programs were still focussing on the murder and the hunt for Kelly's killer. Most theories suggested that a cult could somehow be involved, so they were crammed with so-called experts discussing the likelihood of an underground cult in their community. Hearing them talk about her friend like she was somehow to blame for what had happened made her so angry that she was barely aware of the remote in her hand until she heard the crack. Tossing the broken remote aside, she sighed heavily and decided to venture downstairs. Her footsteps echoed eerily throughout the quiet house. Reaching the kitchen, she found a note explaining that her mum was shopping and would be back soon. The familiar feeling of loneliness washed over her. Since the murder she had felt alienated from her parents and the fact that she was an only child had made her friendship with Kelly even more important. Now she really was alone.

Glancing out the window, the sight of the graveyard made her stomach to lurch. Suddenly the bright sunshine did not permeate the shadows which surrounded her. A sense of foreboding hung in the air. A knock on the door stirred her.

"Hello?" a voice called. Peering around the door was their

elderly neighbour Mrs. Kennedy. She was carrying what looked like a casserole dish.

"Is your mum in?" She chirped. Despite her cheery tone, Amy noticed that Mrs. Kennedy refused to meet her eyes.

"She's out," Amy answered slowly, wondering what the woman wanted. Engaging in friendly chat could lead to the kind of probing questions she wanted to avoid. "She won't be back until later," Amy added, willing the older woman to leave. To her dismay, Mrs. Kennedy came closer, and stood for a moment at one of the wooden chairs surrounding the table.

"I'd love a cup of tea, dear", she said, busying herself with taking out the teacups and sugar.

"Well help yourself", Amy countered "I've got a dentist appointment actually," she mumbled, then quickly stumbled from the kitchen. She didn't care if Mrs. Kennedy thought she was rude, she had an overwhelming desire to escape the suffocating silence of the house.

Outside, the dazzling sunlight temporarily blinded her, and she wandered towards the town without thinking. Since it was a nice day, the streets were crammed with people making the most of the sunshine. The sight of so many carefree people made Amy realise how heavy her burden of grief was. She'd have given anything to laugh and enjoy the day without having to feel guilty.

Gradually she began to notice the staring. Walking past two of her classmates, Amy could feel their stares boring into her back, their whispers following her footsteps. It seemed there would be no escape from misery for her, she was condemned to remember Kelly's murder for the rest of her life. Her gloomy thoughts were disrupted by the sight of what looked like a camera crew on the street. Denied access to the actual murder scene, they had resorted to interviewing locals who were only too glad to offer opinions on the tragedy. It seemed funny to Amy that the first ones to say how stricken they were by the events were the ones who hadn't even known Kelly, who would appear concerned and touched but could soon return to their normal lives.

It wasn't fair, she reflected. Now the day didn't seem so bright. She turned to go home, deeply sensitive to every stare, every comment. People she knew, people she considered equals, even friends, now turned away to mutter behind her back, or worse, blatantly stare at her only turning away when she looked them directly in the eye. Her challenging gaze seemed to embarrass them.

It's bad now, she thought miserably, what will school be like?

Reaching home she was glad to find that Mrs. Kennedy had left, leaving her casserole on the table. She wandered around the kitchen, picking at it occasionally. The day was drawing to a close now, the room gradually beginning to darken. The door opened suddenly, making her start. It was her mum.

"Sorry I'm late!" she called brightly.

Amy remained silent, concentrating on the deepening shadows in the room.

"Why don't you turn the lights on, and I'll heat up the casserole?" Her mother chattered cheerfully then stopped abruptly. Amy was gone, hurrying up the stairs to greet the oncoming night with her troubled thoughts.

Giovanni

James Sheedy
17 yrs, Tullamore Writing Group

ANOTHER PAPERBACK NOVEL. *Another story of romance, of passion, of unconditional love, and happily ever after.*

Damn it, she thought regretfully, breathing heavily through her button-like nose. She sat there in bed, nervous about the night that lay ahead. She threw the book at the wall, the loud thud was surprisingly satisfying, momentarily relieving a fraction of frustration. She started to think about how life should have been, hyperventilating now. She felt love, real love, was the piece missing from the complicated jigsaw that was her life, and she thought she'd found her soul-mate.

She was wrong.

Maybe sorrow is your soul-mate? Stop! Stop being such a fucking drama-queen.

"Why do I always have to be so melodramatic?" she said out loud.

That's it, you're officially losing it!

She hated love clichés but one was true: 'love hurts.' She had trusted someone, forgotten his flaws, told him everything, darkest secrets, insecurities. She had made herself completely vulnerable. She felt hollow now that he had finished it. Hopefully, tonight, they would sort things out.

Somewhere across the vast city was Giovanni. The moonlight blanketed the balcony with an eerie yellow-white glow. Shadows here and there, like odd blotches of paint on a stained canvas. Giovanni sat there, the cancerous fumes of the cigar smoke overpowering the strong stench of the city that lay below, although his other senses reminded him of the chaos of New York. The lights of cars and buildings seemed to stretch to infinity, a beautiful optical illusion of yellows, purples and reds. The lights were alive; flickering, blinking, all independent of each other. Most were moving. The noise was distant yet very evident; he could hear the traffic and general mayhem of the city that never slept. The laughter, screaming sirens, blaring beeps all combined to remind him of where he was. He was one with the raucous yet he felt removed, relaxed even, for the first time since his father was diagnosed. Business had consumed his thoughts for long enough.

Giovanni just sat and waited patiently for the knock at the door, waking himself out of the trance that descended over him now and again when he thought too much about the past, the good times and the bad.

"Life is finally looking up for you, Gio. On the business side anyways."

He always did that, talked to himself in the third person.

"Just don't screw it up now. No time for swelled heads or taking your eye off the Holy Grail."

It was time for some personal shit after three weeks of intensity and paranoia. He was told to wait here by his ex. 'The room where we first made love.' It wasn't just sex; they had taken things slow and after a couple of months consummated their love. That'd been a first for Giovanni, who was a fan of instant gratification. Undoubtedly worth the wait, it was utterly intense yet intimate. How could he forget? The smallest of details were vivid in his memory. For an instant he felt her expensive fruity perfume tickling his nose hairs, not a clue of the name, but it was her smell and it sent him spiralling in to a wavy sea of nostalgic ups and downs.

Instant gratification, Giovanni always got what he wanted. This came with being the son of such a big player in the New York world of organized crime. A god, in many respects, whose name struck fear into the hearts of many powerful and not so powerful people.

His dad always said, "Scare someone enough and they'll do anything. Fear makes people forget about principles, pride, and even phobias."

He always remembered what his dad told him. His hero, his hero was now failing, clinging on to the last shreds left of his life. That's all Giovanni's dad could do now – cling. Hope for a few more moments of happiness before he made the journey to the next life where he would be faced by the wrath of a far superior God. He couldn't blackmail or bully this God into doing things his way. Although knowing his father, he'd try.

If it worked out with her it worked out, if it didn't it didn't.

Who are you kidding, ya flamin' idiot.

She always gave out to him for calling himself names. He sometimes felt like he wanted her more than the thing he had worked and schemed for his whole life. He wanted for her to turn up at his door. Jade, he loved that name, the colour of her brilliant green eyes, speckled with turquoise. Almost six foot tall, and legs that went on forever, hoping she wanted to get back together, to work things through. They always fought, always, but that never ever made him doubt his feelings.

And he didn't usually have feelings that were remotely as strong as love.

She always called him 'Iceberg.' He always smiled when she called him that. He never got her quirky little jokes, but smiled anyway, not a forced smile. He smiled because she was smiling, that million dollar smile that could stop traffic at rush hour in this great city.

A taxi driver had one told her she should "put that mouth to good use, tuts!"

Giovanni had pretended not to care, just smiled at Jade and said, "Hey you can't help it if you're gorgeous."

A wry smile spread across his face.

"...tuts."

She'd slapped him playfully and laughed, soon forgot about the balding, crooked-nose, ignorant yank.

Giovanni didn't forget. He memorized the licence plate

number and the guy's face. Hunted him down the next day and killed him without flinching. That was the hidden side of Giovanni, the side his 'associates' saw. Ruthless, a temper not to be tested, he was almost inhumane at times. Jade brought out whatever human qualities were left in him, because no matter how tough you pretend to be, taking life from another person as you look into their eyes and they plead for mercy effects you deeply. He had regrets, many. He didn't need to kill that guy. Or many others who he'd mercilessly sent to the grave far too early, but the feeling of power and the adrenaline as it pumped throughout him, heightening his senses, hairs standing on end, was intoxicating. He never failed to pull the trigger.

'If you keep regretting the past soon enough the present is gonna come and bite you in the ass.' One of his fathers' favourites.

As he sipped on the fine, fruity Californian rosé wine and just sat there on the cold metal chair and thought of the past, the night he broke up with her, he ran his fingers through his dark hair.

"It's over."

He could still hear her heart break when he said those words, he felt like shit that night, and for many nights afterwards, lower than shit. A mixture of factors made him do it, but he had never regretted anything more. Maybe tonight would be the night to fix that part of his past? Suddenly a splash of red was added to the canvas. Deep in his thoughts, Giovanni felt the hot lead entering his left temple. It was only for a brief moment. His usually expressionless face had never looked more vivified, wrought with pain and a hint of confusion. His short, luxurious life was over. Across the way, in a high class hotel, a light switched off but you could almost hear the smile through the open window.

Beep beep. On the other side of town Jade got a text.

"It's done. Talk tomorrow."

She smiled. She'd played Giovanni at his own game, and

won. She'd learnt from the best. Giovanni's past had just bitten him in the ass. Another love cliché that seemed apt sprang to mind.

'All's fair in love and war.'

Ella

Heather Reid
17 yrs, Kilbeggan Writing Group

– Excerpt –

Ella pulled her headphones from her ears.

"Shit!"

The battery on her MP3 player had died again, right in the middle of her favourite song. She tucked a stray curl behind her ear, dodged a puddle and hopped over the moss-covered wall into the schoolyard. Lauren, came running arms open, "hey," she pulled Ella into a smothering hug.

"You're five minutes late! I thought you were going to wait for Zoë so she wouldn't be late."

Ella smiled to herself. Lauren was such a mother hen always worrying about everybody else.

"She coming. Oh and thanks for the English homework. You're a God send!"

Click, click, click. Zoë swaggered towards them.

Lauren opened and closed her mouth, lost for words.

"Zoë we told you not to wear heels. Your feet will be killing you all day," groaned Ella.

"Yeah well it's a free dress day and I love my shoes. Don't give out to me, anyway, I can't say much about what either of ye are wearing," snapped Zoë.

Ella sighed. She had dressed to keep everyone satisfied, pink Converse to stop Zoë complaining, black blouse to shut Lauren up. It obviously hadn't worked. Lauren didn't like the pink, and Zoë hated her shirt. Ella glanced at Lauren. She was wearing her usual black teamed with black.

Should have worn my red top instead, she thought forlornly following the others into school. The three girls pushed their way down the corridor as the first bell rang in their ears. They were ok for time. The first years were only just leaving their locker room as the girls passed.

"Right what have we first?" Lauren sleepily turned the key in her locker.

"French," Ella replied, fishing out her tech book and a couple of folders for her other classes. She stuffed her books into her already bursting bag.

"Bloody hell," she hugged the bag to her chest and fought her way through the crowds to B1 for double French.

Entering the French room was like going back in time. Carpet tiles still covered the floor although their colour had changed from green to a funny shade of white. The room still contained the ancient wooden desks with chairs attached, which made it impossible to adjust the seat to a perfect napping position. Every student took a fit of sneezing at some point during the class. Mr Quigley refused to allow his chalkboard to be replaced by a dust free white board. He said it was to do with school heritage or something like that. In reality he just liked to see the students suffering.

Mr Quigley came striding into the room and bellowed, "Settle down now class," to an already mute and motionless group of students. At the grand height of five foot two Mr. Quigley felt intimidated by any student who was taller than him. Which basically meant any student from second year upwards. This morning he was on his tippy-toes. A bad sign. He was in an… em… towering temper, although he was wearing his usual Monday shirt. Maybe things weren't so bad after all.

"I have taken it upon myself to photocopy Lauren's homework to show you all exactly how verbs in the past tense are *not* meant to be done."

Oh bloody brilliant, thought Ella. She shot a worried glance at Lauren but Lauren seemed to be taking it in her stride.

"Wonderful," Lauren grinned looking around the class. "It's about time too. I mean you'd think in our sixth year of doing French that we would all be able to do verbs in the past tense but I suppose it *is* a reflection on your teaching abilities."

Everyone craned their heads to see if Mr. Quigley would explode. He clenched his jaw and narrowed his eyes, but that was. Silently everyone knew he didn't kick Lauren out of class because it was a well-known fact that Mr Quigley fancied the geography teacher. And the geography teacher just happened to be Lauren's mother.

"I think detention tomorrow at lunch should do," he hissed.

Lauren's lids flickered; surprised that Quigley dared to punish her. Ella looked down at the photocopied page in front of her. She saw some words. Then her mind drifted. What was she going to do? Where would she get the money? She looked across at Zoë and scribbled a note.

Haircut – Later?

Zoë nodded keeping her eyes fixed on Mr. Quigley.

The next few classes passed pretty uneventfully. At lunch Ella could sense that Lauren and Zoë were looking at her with serious faces. She hated pity. Thank god the lunchroom was crowded. Too crowded to ask Ella about home. No one asking about her life. That was a good thing.

"You ok?" Lauren asked in a meaningful way. Ella smiled and nodded. Zoë seized the opportunity to re-read Lauren's French homework.

"Look, Quigley was right," she said sharply.

"He's a total moran," Lauren snapped.

Mr. Quigley was the worst teacher in the school but Zoë would die before she would hear a bad word against him. She thought he was drop dead gorgeous and if people listened to him they would see what a great teacher he was. Ella and Lauren thought she was mad. Mr. Quigley had the most boring, droning voice in the school. He was severely vertically challenged and balding which, in Ella and Lauren's opinion, was far from attractive.

"I mean what the hell does this word mean anyway?" boiled Lauren. She stabbed her finger at the page as if it was diseased before flinging it back at Zoë and pulling an apple out of her lunch box. She always brought her own lunch. It was a well-known fact that the school food was dangerous after a girl had found chewing gum in her roll at the start of the year.

"Oh that word," Zoë lied her face colouring, "em, I don't know."

"How's it spelled?" Ella cut in, annoyed at being left out. Zoë threw Lauren a killer look but she continued anyway.

"B-u-v-e-u-r," stammered Lauren.

"It means drinker," Ella sighed, taking a sudden interest in a spot of gum on the ceiling. She counted to ten slowly, trying to fight back the lump in her throat. Lauren hung her head in shame. Zoë shot her an I-told-you-so look. Ella hated that her mother infected everything. Even when she wasn't there. Even at school.

"It's fine Lauren. You weren't to know," Ella assured her friend though she bit her lip to stop herself from crying or screaming or both. "Seriously it's fine," she flicked her head away. Thinking of something, anything to change the subject and get away from her mother.

"Look guys lets just focus on Saturday ok?"

"Oh yeah," squealed Zoë, "I'll finally be 18. I'll actually be old enough to drink and smoke and…"

"Do all the things you've been doing since you were 15," finished Lauren disapprovingly. Ella scanned the dining hall. She wondered how many people knew about her mother. How many laughed at her when her back was turned? Then she spotted someone, someone she'd never seen before.

"Stall the ball," said Ella in an impressed, dreamy kind of voice. "New guy. By the door. Only guy in uniform. The principal must have conveniently forgotten to mention it was a free dress day."

"She could have at least told him not to touch those doors or buy food from the shop," Lauren said with a hint of green in her face.

"God he stands out!" burst Zoë.

Is that all you two can think about, thought Ella. He's bloody gorgeous. One of ye notice it please!

"I wonder what classes he's in?" questioned Lauren.

Now that's more like it, Ella smiled. A healthy interest. One of ye isn't going blind!

"Oh who cares," groaned Zoë, playing with her hair.

"I do," whispered Ella softly though neither of them heard.

The Diary

Gill Carmody
17 yrs, Tullamore Writing Group

HE TIPTOED IN. Jenny would kill him if she knew what he had just been dared to do. He peered at his surroundings; each thud of the stairs made his heart thump louder. In all of his eight years he'd never been this scared. The floorboards creaked beneath him as he edged closer to her bed.

"Go on Jack!"

Jack heard his best friend Mick egging him on from the door, too terrified to enter Jack's sister's realm! Jack didn't blame him. Her weeks of washing lay all over the floor and even crawled up her off-white wardrobe like a giant pink snake. Her make-up lay all over a neat little table that she had placed under the window.

"I can't do it, Mick. I just can't. It's too… gross and weird!"

Jack was becoming even more petrified. The room had a presence about it; the smell of girly perfume nearly choked him as he edged towards his older sister's pillow.

"I'm not even sure that it's gonna be here, Mick."

At this stage Jack's hands were trembling uncontrollably. He reached slowly under her pillow and fought his way through the maze that was her pyjamas. Suddenly his hand hit something hard, he knew he had found what he was looking for.

"I got it!" he yelled as he legged it to the door.

Mick let out a short yelp as the two friends squeezed into the large, walk-in closet. Jack turned on the light and there the two boys stood in wonder at what now lay on Jack's pile of boxer shorts.

'My Diary' it read.

"Boy, are we gonna get in trouble for this," Mick whispered.

But despite all the ominous trouble they would have to face from the villainous Jenny the two boys were excited… very excited!

"Let's do this."

Jack licked his lips as he opened the brown, leather cover of his older sister's diary…

"Mammy!"

The shouts could be heard as far as the neighbours house. It had been an hour since the boys had stolen the diary and were still hunched over it engrossed in Jenny's stories about boyfriends and guys who she liked and girls she despised. Now they were in for it.

"Jack, I think we should hide somewhere else, they'll find us in here for sure…"

Mick was starting to have mini-palpitations. He knew that he didn't want to get on the wrong side of Jenny. One time his sister had called Jenny fat and as payback, when his sister had fallen asleep on a school trip, Jenny shaved her eyebrows off!

"I want to go home with eyebrows thanks very much!" Mick blurted suddenly.

Jack made a face, his confused face, but he soon snapped out of that. They needed to find a hiding place and they needed camouflage to get them there.

"Hold on."

Jack reached up on tiptoes to the second shelf and grabbed a bag which had 'SWIMMING GEAR' written on it in block capitals.

"Here, take these."

Jack handed his friend a pair of baby-pink Speedo goggles, he chose a khaki green pair for himself. He then carefully extracted two swimming caps to match the goggles.

"Why do I have to wear the pink ones?"

Mick picked up his 'camouflage' and eyed the goggles in sheer horror. Jack sighed.

"The greeny ones are mine. Those are Jenny's. I'm sorry Mick but I haven't got any others unless you want my daddy's but, to tell you truth, I reckon that his head is twice the size of yours and that wouldn't work!"

So Mick, resigned to the fact that this option would be better than having no camouflage at all followed Jack out of the door and onto the landing. Carefully, the two boys made their way down the stairs. Jack's mother was in the kitchen calming down an overly-put-out Jenny.

"This is so much worse than when he picks his big, slimy nose and rubs it on me... Oh MAMMMY... That is my LIFE... My life... I dunno what to do... Oh my God. This is a catastrophe!"

On hearing Jenny's whinging Jack turned to Mick.

"She does this when she wants to get me into trouble," he whispered. "She uses the 'Mammy' word. I hope that I never grow up to be like that so... What's the word? It begins with 'm'."

Jack knew that his friend would know. Mick knew everything. He was the one who filled Jack in on the whole 'How do we get babies?' question. Mick said that the daddy rubbed his bellybutton against the mammy's and there you go. Jack knew that Mick would grow up to be a scientist, he was so intelligent.

"I think you mean Marijuana. Yes that's it. My sister told me that it's that stuff that makes teenagers all grumpy and stuff."

Jack nodded at his friend's knowledge.

"Yes, well I don't want to be like Marijuana then."

Suddenly, movement could be heard from the kitchen. The two boys, goggles and all, leaped into the living room to avoid being caught. Mick began to tremble. There was no way out.

"Jack... We... We're stuck."

Jack could see that his friend was on the verge of tears. He needed to act quickly. What would his idol James Bond do in this situation?

Jack had a brainwave.

"I know, get the cushions and fire them out the window."

"Out th... th... the window?"

Mick looked as if he needed to vomit. A surge of heat

rushed down through him and suddenly he feared he might wet himself.

"Yes, Mick, out the window. We are going to build a spy den where nobody can see us. Like James Bond! I can be 007 and you... you can be Moneypenny seeing as you've got the proper glasses for the part!"

Jack was surprised that his friend seemed eager about this role. Little did he know but Mick wasn't allowed watch James Bond. It was always on past 8.30, and it had swear words in it, and belly-button rubbing! Suddenly Mick, thinking he had a great role to play, began to feel more comfortable. He might have been the brains of the duo but Jack certainly was the practical one!

The two heaved the huge, cream cushions with wine, intricate petals out of the window and carried them to where the great oak tree stood in the back garden. Here they heaped the cushions to form a square-shaped den in which they could hide.

"Nobody will find us here, 007," Mick exclaimed, happy with himself.

"Moneypenny, time for us to synchronise our watches."

Neither boy had a clue what that meant but they looked at their plastic toy watches on Jack's command. Mick fixed his goggles so as he could see a little better; everything had been pink since he'd put them on in the closet. Jack was hunched down low peeping out a little hole in between two cushions.

"The coast is clear," Jack said matter-of-factly.

No answer.

"I SAID, the coast is clear, Moneypenny... Bond to Moneypenny. Come in."

Still no answer.

Frustrated, Jack turned around to find Mike, pink-goggled eyes facing towards the sky, his mouth wide open like a young bird waiting to be fed by it's mother. There, towering above their spy den was Jenny, a pink razor in her chubby hand...!

Crystle

Andrew Murray
17 yrs, Kilbeggan Writing Group

HIDDEN IN SOCIETY
THAT'S WHAT I WORK TO PREVENT.
I'M A PRIVATE INVESTIGATOR.
I SPECIALISE IN THE SO-CALLED 'WEIRD' CASES.
3
I'M CRYSTLE

I HAVE A SECERT.
I HAVE POWERS.
I AM A WITCH.
I USE MY MAGICK TO HELP SOLVE STRANGE CASES. BUT I'M DRAWING A BLANK ON THIS ONE!
CLANG!
HERALD
10 WOMEN KILLED IN LAST 10 NIGHTS

TEA?
MARK, YOU'RE A STAR
PENS
I KNOW. ANY LUCK WITH THE CASE YET?
NONE SO FAR. THE ANSWER IS RIGHT IN FRONT OF ME. I KNOW IT.
CLICK!
CRYSTLE, YOU'RE THE BEST DETECTIVE THERE IS. YOU'LL GET THE ANSWER, YOU ALWAYS DO.
KETTLE'S ON. I'M GOING FOR A FAG.
RIGHT! BACK TO WORK.

THE ANSWER IS RIGHT IN FRONT OF ME... OH! WAIT A MINUTE!
What is it you wish to see?
SHOW ME ALL TEN VICTIMS' LAST DESTINATION.

He leads her from the place they met.
In stone her dreadful fate is set.
club m
The unforgivable he has stole.
Ancient and evil, absorbing her soul
THANK YOU...

CLUB M? ARE YOU SURE?
PRIVATE INVESTIGATIONS
MURDER AREAS!!
POSITIVE! NO-ONE NOTICED IT BEFORE BECAUSE THEIR ATTENTION WAS ON THE IMMEDIATE MURDER SPOTS - ALL ALLEYS AROUND THE CLUB.
GREAT! CRYSTLE, SEE IF YOU CAN FIND ANY MORE COMMON DENOMINATORS
ALEX, I WANT YOU TO GO TO CLUB M TONIGHT AND CHECK AROUND...
SURE
... I'LL BE EXAMINING THE MURDER SCENES. THERE'S MORE TO THIS THAN WE CAN SEE.

WHY DID I EVEN AGREE TO THIS? CRYSTLE YOU ARE FAR TOO NICE! NOW ALEX IS OFF ON A DATE WITH HER NEW MAN AND YOU'RE STUCK WITH HER SHIFT! OKAY, FOCUS. A PERFECT ENTRANCE IS CRUCIAL FOR GRABBING MALE ATTENTION
AND SMILE. BIG, BIG SMILE!

HI, I'M DAVID. CAN I BUY YOU A DRINK?
I WOULDN'T MIND A BLACK RUSSIAN.
WOW, HE GETS TO THE POINT. SO, HE'S EITHER THE KILLER OR JUST A REGULAR GUY. THAT NARROWS IT DOWN CONSIDERABLY!
SOME TIME LATER...
THAT'S A VERY INTERESTING PENDANT YOU'RE WEARING. IT'S THE AQUARIUS SYMBOL ISN'T IT?
THAT'S RIGHT.
WHY DON'T WE GO SOMEWHERE A LITTLE MORE PRIVATE?

GOD! I AGREED TO LEAVE WITH A GUY I'VE JUST MET, WEARING THESE CLOTHES. I FEEL LIKE SUCH A SL... HUH?
CLANGG!!
GODDESS SHINING BRIGHT, SURROUND ME WITH PROTECTIVE LIGHT!
FZT!
AHHH! MY ARM!
YES, I UNDERSTAND. ONE TO GO!

WHAT? HOW COULD THIS HAVE HAPPENED? ANOTHER WOMAN DEAD. BUT I WAS WITH THE KILLER AT HALF ELEVEN. UNLESS THERE'S MORE THAN ONE KILLER.
SPORT
Another Young
Killed Last Night
continued from page 1.
OH GOD, HOW COULD I HAVE MISSED IT? THAT WOULD EXPLAIN HIM TALKING TO HIMSELF. MAYBE THEY'RE TELEPATHIC?
WHICH MEANS THEY'RE MAGICAL KILLERS, MUCH MORE DANGEROUS THAN I THOUGHT! NOW, WHAT WAS THAT SYMBOL ON THE ATHAME?
CELTIC SYMBOLS
SEARCH
GO
PREV. NEXT.
YES! THIS IS IT.
FIG. 4.

This ancient Celtic symbol belongs to a brotherhood of evil men called "The Order of Rhiannon". Rhiannon being the Celtic god of the underworld (for more see Celtic Gods and Goddesses).
This group was formed around 2000 BC, nearing the end of the stone age, when the symbol was created. The goal of the order is to gain ultimate control over everything. With unlimited power they could bend anything to their will and shape the world in their own vision. One of the main rituals to gain this power involves acquiring the twelve souls of twelve women, each born under one of the twelve zodiac signs. On the third day of the third month with the new moon in the sky, the ritual takes place in the presence of the twelfth victim.
In 1500 BC a powerful witch named Maeve stopped the order, but she couldn´t destroy them completely. They have been dormant ever since, belived extinct by some.

MAEVE
Woodcarving 1500 BC

TODAY IS THE 3RD OF THE 3RD! RUNNING OUT OF TIME. I NEED TEA. I NEED TO THINK.
THEY HAVE ELEVEN OF TWELVE SOULS. THEY GOT AQUARIUS LAST NIGHT. THAT WAS ANOTHER THING THAT SHOULD HAVE TOLD ME. WHAT MAN NOTICES YOUR JEWELERY?
SO THEY NEED PISCES.
HEY, WHAT'S THIS?
GOD, NO! PLEASE NO!
Gone to Club M with David. Be in Late tomorrow. Al!

OKAY, CALM DOWN. YOU COULD BE OVERREACTING. SHE COULD BE DATING ANOTHER DAVID.
WHAT'S THAT?
THAT'S ALEX'S CAR! I WAS RIGHT, I KNEW IT, I KNEW IT!

GOD OF DARKNESS - WE SUMMON AND STIR YOU ON THIS NIGHT. AWAKEN AND ACCEPT THIS FINAL SACRIFICE. BESTOW UPON US...
GET AWAY FROM HER!
FZZZT

OH, MY HEAD. WHAT'S HAPPENING? UGHMMM...
CRYSTLE, CAN YOU HEAR ME?
MAEVE, BUT HOW?
YES, IT'S ME. WE HAVEN'T MUCH TIME YOU ARE MY DESCENDANT. WE MUST WORK FAST AND TOGETHER.
DON'T TRY TO UNDERSTAND THIS NOW. YOU NEED TO TRUST YOUR POWER. REACH DEEP INSIDE YOURSELF. BELIEVE.
NOW TAKE MY HAND. YOU WILL KNOW WHAT TO DO.

LOOK AT WHAT YOU'VE DONE. YOU'VE RUINED IT! RUINED EVERYTHING! YOU'LL PAY FOR YOUR INSOLENCE WITH YOUR LIFE, WITCH.
PUREST MAGICKS ARISE, FREE THESE LOST SOULS INTO THE SKIES. POWERLESS SHALL THESE MEN FOREVER BE AND SEND BACK THE PAIN TO THEM TIMES THREE!
NOOOoo!!

HOW COULD YOU? THE SOULS, THE POWER - IT'S ALL GONE. HOW COULD YOU?
AFTER THE POLICE ARRESTED THE NOW-POWERLESS BROTHERHOOK, I HAD TO COMFORT ALEX AS BEST I COULD.
I DON'T GET IT. WHY WOULD HE DO SUCH A THING? I TRUSTED HIM AND HE ALMOST KILLED ME. AND WHY IS IT EVERY GOOD GUY IN DUBLIN IS EITHER GAY OR MARRIED?
DON'T ASK ME, THE ONLY MEN IN MY LIFE RIGHT NOW ARE BEN AND JERRY! COME ON, IT'S A GIRL'S NIGHT IN.
MY NAME IS CRYSTLE, AND I'M A WITCH. HEY, IT'S A LIVING!

Through Rain and Night

Shane Gillen
17 yrs, Tullamore Writing Group

THE WIND BRINGS her to me. I do not ask it to. She does. Countless nights of rain running down the window creating mini waterfalls. Street light dances through the trickling mini waterfalls, making for skipping shadows on the far wall of my bedroom. The moonlight accompanies the artificial. I'm so far down, away from the sky. I'm so far down. There's nothing left to lift me up.

From her.

To fly me away from her.

That voice whispers through my head again. It has no reason to be there. But it is here. Her voice flies slowly over the hairs on my neck. Every hair stands on end. She has no reason to be here, but she comes when she pleases. She possesses me. She's my torturer. Don't wake up. Keep dreaming. Or she'll hit me. She'll bleach my eyes again. She'll bleed the blue of my eyes away again. I'll cry away each iris.

I had painted up my secrets. I didn't tell anyone about her until it was too late. I never knew her. I never even met her… not under normal circumstances anyway. Sometimes I just wish I could see her, just so I could know where she is. That way I wouldn't be so fearful. I wouldn't be so riddled with this fucking fear if I knew her intentions. If I knew whether or not she'd be coming back. I wonder what it is she wants from me. Sometimes I feel that if I knew, I'd just give it to her, if it would just make her go away.

It all started two years ago. I can't remember how we met. It was through a friend of a friend or something like that. Nothing important. I have vague memories of her appearance – shoulder-length dark hair, distinctive eyes – not because of any beauty or mystery entwined in them, but because of the shape. They were different. I can't explain, her features almost looked Asian, but not quite. Her skin was pale, outstandingly so. She was gaunt, to a *haunting* extent.

Funny I should say that.

No words had been spoken that day. We just happened to be in the same garden, a friend of a friend's, like I said. I felt no attraction towards her. And that was the first time we met. I'm not sure if there was even an introduction. Someone had just told me her name and I presume someone told her mine. Well they had to have because she text me when I returned home that evening, two years ago.

So it began.

I didn't know why she had contacted me. But she had. So I was courteous. I didn't know the hidden truths behind her texts. I didn't know what would become of all this.

But now, as I sit writing this, alone in my bedroom, alone in my house, two years on, I'm riddled with the trauma. I stare out my window, painted with rain from tonight's sky, and I can see her. She stands staring in at me. The other side of the road. She haunts every single raindrop that falls on my roof. I don't know why she's there. But she is. I'm peering from the slit between the blind and the window edge out at my quiet estate, and the girl standing staring at me.

This all started when her texts became a little too incessant. I didn't know her. We weren't even introduced. But she knew my name and I knew hers. That's all she seemed to need. She started to become agitated if I didn't reply to her texts. I didn't know her. What did she expect? All she was was a phone number in my pocket. Not even one in my head – just one stored and saved to a little machine in my pocket. Just a name.

Just a meaningless name.

But a name that kept returning and returning to the screen

of my phone. That beep – when I switched my phone to 'discreet' – that little beep sent chills up my spine.

Those chills are here tonight. I lie in bed. Only an insignificant amount of light creeps and falls in either side of the blind. Otherwise there is total darkness. There is total silence. No, I can hear the rain. I can hear it hitting the tiles above, splashing on the other side of the window. It's dark, I can hear the rain, and it's cold.

My phone wakes up. That little beep makes itself known and light soars up into the room from the screen. It's the beep that gets me. One new message. Somebody is looking to speak with me. Somebody has written to me. I'm no longer alone. I'm no longer in the dark. There is somebody on that little machine lying on my bedside locker. Inches from me. The light from the phone falls back inside the screen. The message is still there. It's still there, hidden in the dark, hiding in the inbox. I'll let it out if I press any button. I'll see it. It'll show itself, if I let it…

I know what's coming.

I turn in the bed and reach for my phone. The rain falls heavier now. As though trying to tell me something. The splashes on the window, they're whispering… The rain on the tiles overhead begins to groan through the roof. It's trying to get to me. To warn me.

As I reach for my phone, there's a second illumination.

The beam is freed once more from the phone to the sound of that little beep. I grab it. I jab the buttons to free the words. Two new messages. I know it's her. I open my inbox. The light of the phone hurts my eyes.

They're both from her. Her name is written clearly on the screen… I know that her words can freeze my heart with fear. But I'm forced to look. I open the first text. No shorthand. There are three words. I read them and I swear to God I heard the rain whisper them on the window…

"I need you."

Tears escape my eyes, in an attempt to save themselves and get away from the fear felt on the inside. Sweat drops have the same idea. The rain whispers again. "I need you." Chills crawl up my legs and spine like spiders, spiders and ants crawling all over me. The rain gets louder overhead. The air grows colder and colder.

"I need you."

But there's another message to read. My heart is trying to beat a little faster. It's trying to tell me not to be scared, but it's scared stiff itself. There's no adrenaline rush. Nothing at all to banish the haunting whispers… The next message is opening. I can still see those three words of the last text. Why does she need me? It's as though she yearns to be a part of me… to possess me… The next message shows itself. Two words. Just two words. Two words can't hurt anyone.

The rain on the tiles groans louder. It begins to thump. The splashes on the window become little knocks, knocking on the window. The new text message glares at me. Once again, I hear the words as I read them.

"Look outside."

One million other words could have been written in that text. But those were the two that she had chosen. I'm no longer alone – am I? There's someone else here now. The rain on the tiles tells me so. It's screaming at me. It's falling on my house, dripping off the side. I know that out there, rain is falling on her too, dripping from her face. I know what I'll see when I look out that window. I've seen it before.

"Look outside."

The words whisper through my head. The spiders carry the whispers with them, through my ears, into my head. I'm afraid that if I close my eyes she'll be there. Will I see her when I dream? I sometimes wonder if she even exists. I wonder if she is even human. I'm not superstitious. But she makes me question what I believe.

I don't know why she screams and cries.

I don't know why she tells me she loves me.

I don't know why she tells me she needs me.

And I don't know why, when I pull my blind aside a tiny bit, she'll be standing there. Lifeless. Is she lifeless? Is it me she needs to possess in order to live? I don't know anything except how she makes me feel. I don't know how she knows what she does. How she knows where I am. Or where I've been. Or who I've been speaking with. If I was to bump into her on the street in the morning I swear to God I would not know her face. That scares me even more. She could be anyone.

So I hear the rain again. The world is crying. I slowly find the strength to lift myself from this bed. I lean towards the window. I know what I'll be faced with. I pull back the blind. The rain is spitting at me, stopped only by the glass. But it's still hitting me hard. I am so cold. I don't know if she can see me looking at her. She's across the road. Soaked from head to toe. I can't make out her features through the night and rain. I can just see that she is wearing dark clothes, that her hair slivers down her face heavy with rain.

Seeing her scares me to the bone. She drains me. She rinses me out. I still see her text. I still hear the rain whisper "I need you"... "Look outside." This is what she wanted; I'm looking outside.

It's been two years since this began.

I know what I'll do next. The same as always. I'll get back into my bed. I'll lie still. And I'll lie in fear of another little beep. I'll spend the night shaking, wondering what it is that she wants. Eventually the night will pass... with or without little beeps. Morning will come, the sun will rise, and she'll no longer be standing across the road.

But she'll return. She won't leave. She haunts me. Soon enough she'll tell me where I've been and who with and it'll start all over again.

As always I'll pray for no little beep.

As always, she'll possess me through night and rain...

The Round Gold Coin

Leanne Geraghty
16 yrs, Kilbeggan Writing Group

BANG. BANG.

"Everybody out", shouted a rough voice. My mother jumped and the small bottle she was using to feed my baby sister Hannah shattered on the wooden floor.

"Oh God, what will become of us?" she whispered. She stood up and silently handed Hannah to me hurriedly packing the few sentimental belongings that we had. I could hear the family upstairs been thrown out as well as the dust from the floorboards flooded our room. My father's eyes gazed steadily at my mother watching her move silently around our small kitchen. She picked up our kettle and threw the contents of it over the fire, it hissed furiously at her. We had only lit it an hour earlier to cook our evening meal on. There was still a good blaze on it before she put it out.

Why has she done that? I wondered. What's going on here?"

The door burst opened. Two men in khaki coloured uniforms marched in. My father jumped up from his chair. I had always considered my father a tall man but he looked small as he spat at the men in uniform to "Get out of my house."

One of them butted him in the stomach with the end of his gun. My mother ran to his side grasping her chest.

"Out", the men ordered. I notice a piece of bread left on the table from our meal. I tried to reach for it but the men had started to knock over the furniture. I watched as the bread came tumbling onto the floor and rolled into the corner, rolling in dust and spiders webs. I was disgusted. My father's wireless came crashing to the floor with a bang, the pieces scattering all across the floor.

"Mammy, what's going on?"

"Nothing dear, be quiet, we have to hurry."

"Where are we going mammy?" I asked full of curiosity.

"Shh, Britta, it's a surprise."

She grabbed our coats in her hand as we left. I didn't understand what was happening. I took one final glance at the small, smoky, messed up kitchen. Hannah started to cry as we walked down the steps to the street. I quickly handed her back to my mother before she really started to scream. The street was full of people.

"Why are we all leaving?" I wondered. Then I notice Mrs Smith from across the road crying. She looked a mess, her grey hair normally tied in a bun was flowing loosely around her shoulders. Mrs. Smith was a widow. I went over to her to ask her, "are you alright?" Hoping that I would get a sweet from her. She always carried a packet of sweets with her.

"Yes dear", she sniffled.

Why was everybody trying to act if there was nothing wrong when clearly there was?

Suddenly Mrs. Smith grabbed me and gave me a tight hug. I will always remember the smell of food from her. She was a great woman for baking scones, brown bread and her speciality queen cakes with chocolate on the top.

"Everything is going to be fine little one," she whispered to me. And with that she handed me a round gold coin. It sparkled as the streetlights caught its glow. I was overjoyed, it felt like Christmas and my birthday had all come at once. I stammered thank you, to her. I couldn't believe it.

Two dark green lorries came flooding into the street and more men in uniform appeared. The men began to shout at us to hurry up. They bundled us into lorries. My mother started calling me frantically. I could see her mass of red curly hair as she searched for me. I ran to her, only for her to hit my hand for running off. I tried to explain that I was with Mrs Smith but she wouldn't listen to me. I swelled up with anger. I decided that I wouldn't tell her about the money Mrs Smith had given me. My father picked me up in his arms as we entered the back of one of the lorries. There was very little space in there. Everyone was squashed together. Once there was no one left on the street, they closed up the doors and we were launched into darkness. I began to think about what I could buy with the money. Maybe three lollipops, or a piece of chocolate, or maybe an aeroplane? It was very hot and clammy in the lorry and tiredness washed over me. I snuggled into my daddy's shoulder and the gentle vibrations of the lorry rocked me to sleep.

Later I awoke when the lorry hit a huge hole making everything jolt. I nearly fell of my daddy's lap.

"Where are we?" I murmured.

"Shush," daddy kissed the top of my head. Hours later the lorry came to a halt. We climbed out. The night was cold and it had begun to rain. My mother help me put my coat to put on. I could hear a steam engine near-by and I began to get excited. I had never been on a train before. There were people everywhere. Babies and toddlers were crying. There were bags scattered all over the place. My mother gave me the bag she had brought with us so it wouldn't get mislaid among the crowd. There were many men in uniforms just standing on the spot. None of them smiling. Then my father did something strange. I watched him walk to a soldier.

"Please have mercy on my children," he pleaded. "They have their whole lives in front of them."

"If your not careful, I'll make sure they don't have the rest of the night in front of them," the soldier snarled.

"What's daddy doing talking to that man?" I asked my mother.

"That man wasn't very good so daddy is just trying to help him to be better behaved so he won't go to hell."

"Oh".

Daddy walked back with his head down, hiding his face.

"Cheer up Daddy", I piped.

He gave me a small smile as if to thank me.

Why was everybody so unhappy? What is happening?

Someone fired shots into the air. Everyone went quiet as stone. Not even a baby cried. A soldier stood up on a tall platform in front of us. He had a piece of paper in his hand and he began to read from it.

"All women, girls and children under the age of five are to board this train. Men and boys re-board the lorries."

People started screaming. Hannah began to cry because of the noise. I grabbed my mammy's hand.

"What's happening, mammy, what's happening?"

But mammy was crying. Her hand grasped my father's neck and she was crying.

"I have to go," Dad hunkered down beside me.

"Where?" I asked, my stomach churning.

"You don't worry poppet." He scooped me up into his arms. He smelt of tobacco.

"Don't go," I begged tears streamed.

"Shh, shhush," dad whispered, "remember to be good for your mammy and help her and your sister. I'll always be thinking of you."

This made me cry even more. I held on tight. But dad prized my fingers away. Mrs Smith came over and took Hannah off my mother so that she could say goodbye to my father. I sat on the ground bawling. Mrs Smith tried to comfort me, but as she was holding Hannah it was hard for her.

What was I going to do without him?

The soldiers came, ripping my father from my mother's arms. I ran and grabbed the tail of dad's coat and held on tight.

"Don't go, don't go, don't go," I cried over and over.

My mother swooped in and picked me up.

"Why cant daddy come with us?" I sobbed.

"Hush Britta, you need to be quite now, show Hannah how quite you can be," my mammy said softly. She squeezed me tight as I kicked and screamed to get back to my daddy. She took one look back at him before climbing up into the train. Mrs Smith walked on behind us with Hannah. All my excitement of going on a train had died out. My mother placed me on the floor. There were no seats. She took the bag off my back, sifted through it, pulled out my father's hat and placed it on my head.

"You mind this for your daddy," she said quietly to me.

The floor was covered in hay and sawdust. We huddled close to keep warm. The doors of the train were shut and we were plunged into total darkness. We sat like this for days and we weren't fed. Luckily Mrs Smith had brought some food with her. I was so glad someone had thought of their stomach. The floor got hard and parts of me went numb. A bad smell started to arise in the carriage. I asked my Mother what it was, but she said she didn't know. Mrs Smith got up during the journey. She didn't come back. It was too dark to go and look for her.

"Where is she?" I asked mammy over and over.

"She couldn't see to come back," mammy told me.

When the doors opened light flooded into the carriage. I put my hands quickly over my eyes to stop the sunlight hurting. When my eyes adjusted I could see that people had been sick all over the place. That was part of what we could the smell. People began to leave the train. When we got out we waited for Mrs Smith. She didn't come. Mammy told me to mind Hannah and our bag of belongings.

"Ill go and get her. You wait here."

Mammy came back out crying with a bag in her hand, Mrs. Smith's bag.

"Where's Mrs Smith Mammy?" I asked wondering why she was crying. She told me that Mrs Smith was going to follow us on after, because she wasn't feeling well and was going to see a doctor.

We were told to move on. We had to walk miles. We walked it in silence. Every person thinking to themselves. I prayed for Mrs Smith that she was happy in heaven and also for my Daddy, hoping that one day we would be together again. We came to big, tall fences that stretched for miles and miles.

Looking through them I saw loads of women digging a big hole.

"What are they doing that for?" I asked. "They're looking for buried treasure honey" my mother informed me. Then I looked just past the women. I saw a strange white mound. At first I didn't know what it was. Then I saw hands. Arms and hands and legs. Mounds of bodies piled on the ground .

"Mammy," I pointed.

"Don't look," my mother's hand blocked my eyes.

We came to an iron archway. An entrance. Inside were cabins. Loads and loads of cabins. Me and mammy and Hannah were brought into a room and given a bottom bunk to share between the three of us. The blanket we had was old and it hurt when it rubbed against my skin. I couldn't stop myself from thinking about my own blanket at home. Everyone in the room was told.

"Your duties are to help with the ploughing and the sowing."

We were woken the next morning at 5.30am by a loud siren. We made our way out to the fields and remained there until noon. We went back to the cabins then and were given a bowl of porridge. This was our meal for the day. Many people protested at this, they said that they're growing children needed more then a bowl of porridge a day. After this we went back to the fields to finish off our work. At 6pm we had an hour exercise time. Mammy helped a woman who had big blotches on her back to wash herself, to help keep the blotches away. At night I was so hungry that I began to eat spiders and other types of insects, I couldn't help it, I was just so hungry. I pretended that they were my favourite biscuit. I never told mammy though. I was afraid she might give out to me or even worse take them for herself.

Every night I prayed for my daddy and I hoped that he was well. Night was bad. I could always hear people crying. Mammy told me they cried because they were lonely. I couldn't understand why because there were more than enough people here so no one should feel lonely. Others screamed in the middle of the night. I had nightmares about the pile of bodies I had seen on the way in to this awful place. I was so afraid that I would end up there. Mrs Smith never followed us on as my mammy had said she would. Mammy said that she might have gotten a job in the hospital that she went to because she was such a nice person. I always kept Mrs Smith's coin in my sock and my daddy's hat in my pocket. New people came and others died of disease or were shot for disobeying the soldiers. Mammy said that these people had gone to their eternal rest, which meant that they would never wake up. Others used this as an opportunity to borrow the dead persons shoes and socks and other bits and pieces that belonged to them. My mother always told me that I shouldn't get too close to people as one day I could wake up and they could be gone.

My eight birthday came and went but I never realised it.

Time had no meaning for us.

Then one morning there was no siren. When we woke up there was no soldiers. *"What was going on now?"*

People began to shriek with joy and happiness.

"The soldiers are gone!"

For the first time in months I heard people laughing. I even laughed myself at a joke someone made, but I didn't understand it. It felt so good to laugh. Within a few hours white trucks came flooding to the camp. They had American soldiers on them. They asked us if we would get on to the trucks to be brought back home.

Home.

When I got out of the truck I looked around. This was where we had boarded the Nazi train. The building where I had heard the men laughing was in ruins. I was pushed and shoved around as people dropped all their belongings to rush to their relatives and friends. My bag was kicked into the air and the belongings scattered about the ground.

"Quick honey, pick them up before they get trampled on", my mother said to me. As I began to retrieve our belongings I heard somebody call my name.

"Britta. Britta."

I looked around.

Daddy!

I ran to him. He scooped me up in his arms. I patted his face, just to make sure he was really there! Mammy started calling my name frantically. She caught sight of me and then her eyes fell upon my daddy's face. She stood and stared at us for what seemed like ages. Then she started running. Running and crying. Holding Hannah close. She collided into us with an almighty force. I cried I was so happy. All my praying to God had paid off. A solider called out for hush and we fell silent.

"Hitler is dead," he roared. "He killed himself last week. Germany is free."

It was the 8th of May 1945.

Early Morning

Fiona O'Malley
17 yrs, Tullamore Writing Group

THE RED TIN shed was filled with the smell of manure as loud groans and moos erupted under a velvety, moonlit sky. An old man's rough, cracked hands stroked a large, black and white cow, as its eyes bulged and its hind legs kicked out, unsettling dust and hay. The old man's forehead creased, showing many wrinkles and deep frown marks.

"Paddy," he said in a hoarse voice, "we'll have to do this ourselves."

"Ourselves?" said Paddy, a tall teenager, in a high-pitched voice, "But sure, the vet'll be back tomorrow!"

"She can't wait lad!"

Paddy rocked on the balls of his feet as he watched his father trying to make the cow comfortable. The old man's tweed peaked hat fell sideways on his head as he sat on a milking stool, revealing a bald patch in his grey, matted hair and casting a shadow over his heavily lined face.

The old man pulled his woollen jumper tightly around his chest, feeling the pinch of the unmerciful winds outside, as he paced up and down the shabby tin shed, his mud-covered wellies slapping off the moist, concrete ground and echoing around him. He looked out the wooden, creaking door, as it moved to and fro, and saw a ripple run through the long grass and field of oats, as the almighty chestnut tree bowed and swayed in the wind.

He lit his pipe, the tiny flame on top of the matchstick quivering, illuminating a bead of sweat rolling down the side of his face, as he looked at his fat cow with concern and anxiety. The light smoke wrapped itself around him, serpent-like, giving him the appearance of a super-natural being or some brave hero.

"She'll be alright, won't she, Da?" he asked.

"Don't be stupid, of course she will!" the old man replied, his voice shaking.

He bent down beside the cow's hind legs and felt her bristly, wiry hair, as he gently shushed her.

Paddy looked out the heavy door and realised that the sky was changing and becoming lighter, as the winking stars were saying their last goodbyes. He could see the leaves dancing and spinning on the concrete as the wind whistled and hummed through the wild ditches and shrubs.

"Paddy, go inside and bring us out a strong cup of tea and a few biscuits, good lad," said the old man, before blessing himself.

Paddy pushed the old door back and felt the wind biting against his ears and tearing at his face. He squinted as he walked, with his back hunched, into the porch of a white-washed farmhouse.

A lantern flickered in the narrow, familiar hallway, as the smell of musk and dampness filled the air. He made his way into the kitchen, his head bent under the low ceiling and his feet shuffling on the jagged flagstones. He twisted a stiff tap, and the water echoed against the belly of an orange, copper kettle. It screeched as he placed it on a piping hot stove.

Paddy sat on a wicker stool and watched as flames licked the stove's glass face, enjoying his moment of warmth and rest.

Fingers shaking, he opened a packet of Figrolls, as his eyes darted around the room, searching for the nearest plate.

Moments later, he walked across the yard, holding a cup of tea and a saucer. The steam from the tea gently brushed against his face, as he saw the sun rising, bursting through the fields and realised that the wind had stopped.

The door creaked as Paddy opened it and saw his father, in one swift move, pull out a wet, baby calf from the rear-end of it's mother. The cup and saucer smashed when it hit the ground, sending biscuits and tea everywhere, as Paddy collapsed on the moist concrete.

The old man's hearty laugh rang out as his tense face broke into a smile, when he saw the calf's knobbly knees wobbling as she made her first steps.

"Ah, sure, would you look!" the old man said to himself. "It's already morning!"

The Turquoise Necklace

Helena Hayes
13 yrs, Kilbeggan Writing Group

I LOOKED INTO the deep blue surface of the cold, icy water. I saw a pale unhappy girl staring back at me.

A soft voice called me from the distance.

"Grace? Grace?" my Mum repeated. "Did you hear what I said, come on inside. It's getting cold."

She disappeared back inside the house.

I closed my eyes. I didn't want to move.

I turned around and headed up the sloping hill. I peered over my shoulder and observed the lake. To the left there stood a tiny island surrounded by trees. According to my Grandfather, in the center of the island there was supposed to be an enchanted cave. He used to tell us stories about how it would glow at night. We all said we never really believed him, but every single one of us was curious. We planned endless secret trips out to the island but always chickened out at the last minute.

My fingertips began to sting as I entered the warm house. The whole family was sitting around the flickering fire. My mother was slumped in her chair reading her book held open with two outstretched fingers in the shape of a v. My father was perched on a stool in the corner glaring at the tiny portable telly munching his way through a bumper value packet of scoffee toffees. As usual my sister got the luxury of the large couch in the corner.

My sister can do no wrong, according to my father, he thinks she will become a businesswoman some day and earn loads of money. He thinks I've got no more brains than a donkey and will probably end up working in a little corner shop. I'll show him. He also has a way of looking at me, at the results of my misdeeds, then at me, as though he was looking directly into my sinful soul.

I floated up the stairs that evening as if not real. I didn't feel real any more.

That morning when I awoke I knew that my world was somehow altered. The orange glow of my alarm clock showed it was still an hour until my usual wake-up call. I just lay there, trying to figure out the change. It was dark but not as dark as it should be. Across the bedroom I could clearly make out the dull glint of my CD player. It stood proudly in the center of my cluttered shelves and above it the looming faces of rock stars I had once thought I should care about. I slipped out from the bedclothes and tiptoed across the creaking floorboards over to the window. A single star shone in a wedge of deep blue above the woods. The wind gently drifted over the lake, creating a small wave. I could see nothing unusual outside.

I pulled on my pink fleece and tiptoed barefoot quietly down the stairs, wincing every time I stepped on a creaking floorboard. I was terrified I would wake my dad. If he woke and found me climbing down the stairs at 6 a.m. it would turn into interrogation time.

When I arrived at the kitchen door I found my dad looking gloomily over the rim of a steaming coffee cup. He didn't say anything. He just continued staring out the window as if in a trance.

"Dad?" I called softly, "what are you looking at?"

I knew it was risky asking him, but curiosity seemed to conquer my fear. I stood in the doorway waiting for a reply or even to be told off but nothing happened. I cautiously took a step towards him, well a half step.

Nothing happened.

The grim look he had on his face that morning made me wonder what image or thought preoccupied him.

I walked over to the old smudged kitchen window and peered out. Outside, a fine grey March mist floated across the lake, but from time to time it parted and I could see the reflection of the moon on the water. The small candle on the windowsill beside me flickered inside its glass holder and made me forget about the chill that had wrapped itself around the house only a few days earlier.

I perched myself on the tiny windowsill and continued staring out. From this window I had a clear view of the small island in the lake. I had never really thought that the island was somehow special, I just thought that my Granddad was going mad. Dad always told us not to believe him, but maybe Dad had something to hide.

I have to go out there, I thought, as I squinted, trying to get a closer look. Tomorrow morning when everyone's asleep, I'll go. I quickly glanced over to where Dad was sitting; he still didn't seem to notice I was there. I promptly got up and headed up to my room before it was too late.

Next morning I got dressed quickly. The light outside my room was still on. The silence that filled the house made me feel unsure. I tiptoed in my socks passed my mum and dads door. I pressed my ear up against the door and listened intently, the soft snoring I heard was somewhat reassuring. When I got to the kitchen, I poured a glass of milk and drank it in one tilt. I went through the passageway by the back door where we kept the coats and muddy boots. I put on my fleece jacket and slipped on my old wellies. I zipped my jacket up to my neck and pulled on my gloves. I opened the door and stepped out into the freezing air and headed down the sloping hill towards the lake.

Even though the sun had yet to show I could clearly see the little boat. My dad bought it last summer; no one had gotten into it since. I just hoped it wouldn't sink. I untied it and pushed out along the pebbles into the shallow water. I hauled myself in and perched myself on the decomposing bench in the center. I grabbed an oar and started rowing. By now the sun was beginning to rise. Various shades of pink and orange crept onto the horizon.

My stomach began to churn. It felt like a little dog was inside chasing its tail partially because of the excitement of going to see for myself what was on the island and partially because I was worried there was nothing there. The closer I got to the island the more I doubted I would find anything. I felt like I was just setting myself up for failure. I always did that. For some reason though this felt different. This time I thought there was really something there.

As I approached the island I could hear stones grating off the bottom of the boat. I climbed down to the stern and cautiously jumped out. The water splashed up and soaked my clothes. I pulled the boat up onto the grass and tied the rope around the branch of a tree.

This is it.

For an hour I rambled around the island, looking for anything, finding nothing. Then I saw it. I carefully choose my steps leading through the trees. I took a deep breath but this time excitement filled my lungs. There was a half-built tree house before me. I walked over to it. One of the walls was on the ground. It must have given in many years ago. Grass grew between the planks of wood. I put my foot on it and it crumbled. A yellow torch was lying close to the wall of the tree house. I picked it up and flicked the switch but nothing happened. I dropped it and climbed into the tree house.

The floor was covered in scrap carpet. In one corner there were a dozen pots of tester paint. The remaining walls were covered in outrageous orange and perfect pinks. In the center of the tree house there was an old kettle, three rusted spoons, two glasses and the remains of an old cup. I took a step forward and tripped over an old sculpture. It looked like a holy sculpture. I couldn't understand why it was there. It didn't make sense that the children who made the tree house would have brought this out. Tears welled up in my eyes. I didn't fight them off. I just cried. Not because of the broken sculpture but because of the disappointment and because this trip hadn't answered any questions, it just left me with more.

I sat down on the uneven ground beside the broken sculpture. I peeled the wet gloves off my freezing hands. I clasped my hands together and dug my nails into the numb flesh until four trickles of blood ran down each hand. I had to feel it. I had no desire to leave, just sit there and fantasise about having a complete understanding of it all.

A final truth.

A clarity.

I dropped my eyes to the rough ground and clumsily got to my feet. A soft breeze blew through the trees creating a rustling noise. Shafts of light flooded through the leaves. I took a giant step over some branches. Twigs snapped under my feet. The cracking echoed and then I realized that the leaves weren't rustling anymore. I stood for a second, letting the silence grow around me. Something didn't feel right. I listened.

At last I continued walking. I walked out through the thickness of the trees. Light flooded around me, it was only then I realized how dark it was in there. I untied the boat rope and once again pushed the boat out along the stones into the water and began my journey back across the lake. I looked down at my feet. A small pool of water had accumulated around the bottom of the boat. The water was gently trickling through a hole. I dug into my pocket and pulled out one of my wet gloves. I wedged part of the material into the hole and the water instantly stopped flowing. As I pulled the tiny boat up onto the grass, I realized that life doesn't hold any answers, just a series of questions.

I sat cross-legged on the soft silky surface of my duvet cover. I rocked back and forth in the darkness. I hummed. I didn't know what I was humming I just hummed. I tried not to let any thought sneak into my mind. I could hear the constant droning of the neighbours from downstairs. You'd think they would leave us alone at a time like this. Since yesterday morning they've been ploughing over with their casseroles and apple pies.

My bedroom door was slightly open, a wedge of light flooded in from the landing. I could hear footsteps approaching. They stopped outside my bedroom door.

"Grace, are you in there?" my sister asked in an emotionless whisper.

"Yes," I replied getting up from my bed.

"Dad wants to see you," she said, instantly walking away.

I didn't understand why he wanted to see me. He didn't have any time for me before. I thought this wouldn't be any different.

I gently knocked on the hard wooden surface of the door. I grasped the cold metal handle with my right hand. Inside my dad lay limply in his bed. His face was seized with pain. His skin matched his hair. A pale grey colour. He looked so weak. I always saw my father as a strong figure in my life, but seeing him so helpless made me unsafe. The bedroom was bathed in pale light. A turquoise necklace was draped across his left hand. My mother sat on his right side, fussing over him. I walked over and sat beside him. He tilted his head in my direction until his eyes matched up with mine.

"I saw you out there that morning," he whispered weakly. "The island. I know you'll do the right thing. Keep searching."

He handed me the turquoise necklace. He closed my hand around it and softly squeezed.

"I love you," I mumbled as the tears rolled down my face.

A smile flickered in the corner of his mouth and quickly died again. He gently leaned over and placed a soft kiss on my forehead.

"Don't be afraid," he said and suddenly I wasn't.

From then on I knew that life did hold the answers. I just had to keep searching, for deep in those dark still waters something shimmered and would some day emerge...

The King of Diamonds

Mary-Kate Wille
17 yrs, Kilbeggan Writing Group

– EXCERPT –

Great! Jane thought as she opened Star's stable door. Filthy again.

She stepped into the stable, put the head collar on her top horse and tied him up outside. As she went to the tack room to collect her grooming kit the shrill ring of the phone echoed across the still yard. The noise made Jane jump.

Who'd be calling this early in the morning, she wondered glancing at her watch? It was only half past seven. She started to run to the office to answer the call, not knowning that it would lead to a series of life changing events. As she emerged from the office, she recalled the conversation. How on earth did that happen? She asked herself. She couldn't help but smile. This could be the answer to her prayers.

"What are you smiling at?" Marie asked cheerily. Jane threw herself at her bewildered cousin and engulfed her in a bear hug.

"You'll never guess what!" she said enthusiastically. "Fredrigo Stillman just called and asked me to train his new four year old!" Jane twirled and looked at the amazement in Marie's eyes.

"No way"

"Yes way!" Jane said as she began dancing around. She filled Marie in with all the glorious details of the up and coming star that would be living at their yard. King of Diamonds was a 16.2HH Hanovarianx thoroughbred stallion sired by an Olympic winner. The horse had been rejected by several people due to its fiery temperament, it had been labled as "dangerous." But Fredrigo saw past this and saw potential in the temperamental colt, believing that one day The King of Diamonds would become a top class horse.

"Surely the animal can't be that bad, can he?" Marie asked her still disbelieving cousin.

"He'll be fine with us," Jane replied in a dazed sort of way.

"I wonder what colour he is?" Marie queried.

"Guess we'll have to wait and see," Jane grinned as she imagined a bright bay horse, neck arched, prancing around a show ground.

"So when's he coming?" Marie's voice was beginning to return to normal now. "Next week!" Jane laughed as Marie's face grew stunned again. "Wednesday. Come on we better get to work, it's Jack's day off so we're in for a busy day."

Jane went back to were she dropped the grooming kit, collected it, and carried on to were Star was standing patiently outside his stable.

"Hey boy," she murmured as she ran her hand along his neck, sighing lightly. "What am I going to do with you, eh?"

Where there would normally be a mane lying across his neck, Star was bare. His mane had to be hogged so that he would be more comfortable. There were several bald patches on each side of his neck. Star had a skin condition called sweet itch, which was an allergy to certain flies. Hopefully King of Diamonds won't have sweet itch, Jane thought. Stop it, what are the chances of that? The voice in her head fought off her worries and she forced herself on brushing the mud off Star's back.

"There, all done!" she exclaimed after picking out Star's hooves. "Right. I'll be back in a minute." Once Jane got into the tack room, she dumped the grooming kit in a corner and opened the medical cupboard. As she picked up the fly repellent, she noted that it was almost empty, and would need replacing. She headed back to Star prepared for a fuss. And sure enough with the first spray, Star began dancing around.

"Easy boy, stand now." She managed to spray him completely without getting trodden on. For once, Jane thought.

"Good boy!" she praised. "Now stay there while I get your tack."

Several minutes later, Jane returned from the tack room and placed the saddle on Star's stable door.

"Come on, open up," she said as she guided the bit into Star's mouth. She closed up the throat lash and nose-band and noticed that the bridle had been cleaned. She made a note to thank Jack the next day. Jane then picked up the saddle and gently placed it on Star's withers, before sliding it into into its correct place. She did up her girth and fastened her hat. She mounted and gave Star a pat.

"Walk on," Jane said and headed out the gates for a gentle hack.

After trotting down the road for a while, Jane pulled up and tightened her girth. She then took a left turn, down a dusty track, were it was safe to canter.

"Now, let's just take it nice and easy OK?"

She nudged Star with her heels. Star leapt forward and got into an even rhythm after a few strides of canter, seeing a fallen log ahead of her, Jane eased Star up and slowed to a trot. Jane looked closely at it to make sure it was safe to jump.

"What d'you think boy? You up for it?" She trotted away from the log and then turned Star around. She pushed the gelding into a collected canter and headed straight for the log.

"Three, two, one…" Star pricked his ears and soared over the jump easily. "Good boy!" Jane laughed patting him on the neck. She let him canter on down the track.

An hour later Star clattered into the yard. Jane dismounted and gave him a mint. "You two look like you had fun!"

Jane turned to see Marie coming towards her.

"We did! Star was brilliant. He's in top form."

Marie smiled and offered to take Star to his stable and rub him down.

"Thanks," Jane said gratefully and headed towards the house to get a much needed drink. As she walked, she saw that Merrylegs was turned out in the arena for some exercise. The little chestnut pony was cantering around giving an occasional buck. She was here to be trained and still had a long way to go. Jane smiled as she thought of the fiery temperament so often associated with chestnut mare's.

Maybe the King of Diamonds is chestnut, she thought her heart jumping, I'll know on Wednesday, she told herself.

Crimson Snow

Darragh Kelly
17 yrs, Tullamore Writing Group

GREG'S FINGERS HAD gone numb. He walked the same route that he always walked. He could do it in his sleep. It was freezing. The weather forecast had said it would be minus five all day, but what they'd forgotten to mention was the wind-chill factor, which made it nearly twice as cold. As he looked up he could see the air forming in front of him. He walked on, bent over, bearing the brunt of the force, the wind cutting at his face like a knife.

Something landed on his shoulder. A snowflake. Greg looked up, watching for a few seconds, waiting in a trance. He shook the snowflake off and ploughed on, his lips now blue from the cold. After five minutes he could feel the snowflakes melting in his hair. He had walked out of his house with his coat, his long scarf but no hat, how irregular of him. He pondered on it. Why had he left his hat behind?

It's not like me to forget, he thought.

It wasn't where he'd last left it. Greg would worry about that later on.

Life for Greg was monotonous. Up at seven after yet another sleepless night. He would drag himself into the shower, which energised him for a while, never for long. He would get dressed. Breakfast. Then out by eight for his morning walk. Of course that was after Greg had made sure over and over that each door and window was locked.

He glanced at his watch. Eight-fifteen. She was late. He took up his vantage point and waited. He would wait all day just to see her.

As time passed his legs began to cramp. The cold cut through him. He wondered if he'd frozen solid. He didn't seem to realise, that blinded by his obsession he was being slowly turned into a human snowman.

She came out of the house. Greg's heart flickered. She was an angel. Every move deliberate, yet so graceful. It was her nature. She crossed the garden in four powerful strides, her dark brown hair waving behind, untouched by the snow. That was what he had come to see. She was a drug. Her beauty inescapable. She was heaven. Yet he wasn't able to get any closer.

The restraining order of course.

Greg turned and left, off to work as always. He was an hour late but his boss, Dave didn't know. Dave was always busy, away at meetings or travelling abroad, he was rarely at the office. Greg sat down on his comfy, squashy chair and quickly pulled out some paper work to make it look like he was busy. His mind was elsewhere, still enmeshed in her world. The way she walked. The way her hair flew back away from the wind. He sat there grinning, his day filling his grey day. Hours passed and still he hadn't moved, not once. He sat motionless, ignoring his stomach, ignoring the hunger pangs screaming at him to get some food. He glanced at the face of his watch. Everything blurred. He rose from his seat his legs aching, willing him to sit down. He was weak. Greg tried to remember the last time he'd eaten. Days ago, he shrugged. He was used to the stomach cramps. He briskly pulled on his coat, pulled the door shut and marched down the corridor. Colliding past work colleagues like a bowling ball through pins. His heart raced. A fine sheen of sweat clung to his skin. He began to panic. He had to see her. He just had to.

Greg walked briskly, nearly jogging. The snow so deep it soaked into his shoes drenching his socks and feet, but that didn't matter he had to hurry, otherwise he'd miss her completely. His hands were freezing, so cold. He took his spot overlooking the river and the trench of houses on the other side. Six o'clock. He had five minutes to spare. He was out of breath, his gut wrenching with hunger. He promised himself to eat something, another promise to be broken.

A taxi pulled up outside of his angel's house, the snow melting on the bonnet. She stepped out. He knew she'd have more sense than to walk home. She paid the driver. He took off hastily. She stood there serenely while the elements obeyed her. The wind swirled around her, the snow never getting close enough to touch her. She was smiling, that heavenly smile, the one that would warm the heart of a statue.

* * *

Greg walked through his front door and shook the snowflakes from his hair. He placed his wet jacket on the banister. Glancing upwards he saw his other half glaring at him with those red piercing eyes.

"So, Greg, you've been watching Helen all day again I gather."

Greg looked down, his body full of shame.

"You're pathetic, you know that. You're pathetic."

The words hung in the air, stinging Greg's ears.

He moved into the corridor making his way to the kitchen. He stopped and looked again.

"And I suppose you didn't do an ounce of work either. You're lazy, lazy and sick. I don't know what is wrong with you. Helen doesn't want to know you. She hates you. I hate you. Look what you've done to yourself. To me."

Greg waited. Every word cut through him with heart breaking pain. He got this every day. The same abuse, every single day, over and over and over.

"Look at me. Look at me. Why are you looking down? Why are you even here? Look at you, you're worthless. You can't work. You can't even feed yourself. You look like a corpse. You are a corpse. You need a haircut. It's down to your bloody shoulders now. You're so pale. You're whiter than milk. Look at your eyes they're like two piss holes in the snow. Oh my god, you're so skinny. I'm surprised you even had the strength to stand. You are such a disappointment. You disgust me."

Greg looked up, exhausted. "Are you finished?" The question lingered. His other half turned away.

"Get out of my sight you disgusting animal."

With that Greg turned away from the mirror, straight into the sitting room for some peace.

In the dead of night his breathing was heavy. He glanced at his watch, green in the black. Four o'clock. Lonely cares drove by, drivers dozing. It was late but not for him.

Walking was easier than dreaming.

As he approached the bridge no one was about and he knew the heavy blizzard would cover his footprints left in the sludge on the ground.

Greg rested at the top of the bridge. The night was so cold. He felt sharp pains in his chest, like the air itself was scarring his lungs with every breath he took. Gazing into the river below, a thin layer of ice had managed to form over the strong current. Greg's head began to spin. Lack of water, lack of food, lack of sanity had left him a shadow. A shadow that passed unnoticed everywhere it went.

Looking down at the river he saw his other half. Terrified he spun away. Shouting filled his ears. Pain and fear streamed through his body. His other half had a profound effect on him. Greg staggered to a pole. He looked like some poor drunk-fool that had lost his way home.

Greg just held on, panting and choking up remnants of spittle and blood. The snow began to pour. Turning his black jacket and black pants into a chequered flag. Time passed and Greed soothed himself by humming and repetitively stroking his nose with his finger. At last he could stand up. He left the pole and walked through the storm following the streets left and right then straight. He could feel the force of the wind pushing and pressing him on. Greg enjoyed the help but that quickly turned to hate and pain. The jacket was absorbing all the moisture behind him. Hunched over he continued loosing all feeling in his back.

There it was. Helen's house. A spacious house, way too spacious for just one person. A small front garden. Greg walked by it and sharply turned down the side of the house nearly slipping on some ice. He got to the side fence door. Clambered up. The wind and cold playing with him, pushing and pulling him backwards and forwards. Twice he nearly fell. Regaining composure, he leapt over and landed rolling on the small pavement. His strength had evaporated. Sweat was seeping out and snow was soaking in. Slowly and carefully he picked himself up.

This had to be done.

He had to do this.

He got to the back door, reached up, stretched his arm out and pulled down a key, which was sellotaped to the frame. Unnoticeable unless shown, he knew all too well that it had been there. He warmed the key between his hands, placed it in the lock and turned. The lock opened without a sound. The kitchen was in utter darkness. Greg stumbled around, fingers feeling nothing, too numb to feel. Light flashed on. Black and white tiles dress the kitchen and the utility room, elegant yet simple.

Greg had dragged mud, snow and the cold in, but soon that wouldn't matter. Searching for mirrors, his eyes danced and rolled crazily in the sockets. He took off his boots, moving noiselessly through the dry hallway, painted cream and up the stairs.

The main bathroom straight ahead, light on with the door wide open. To the left a spare bedroom, blackened with no sign of life. Another left. Helen's bedroom. Cream. The door ajar, with a reading lamp on which gave the room a strange glow. He could hear her breathing softly.

Spreading his weight evenly on both feet he approached and slowly crept inside. She was sprawled on her tummy, hair lying across her back. She appeared to be wearing nothing, only beauty and grace. A smile spread across Greg's lips. He walked over to the big, old mahogany, chest of drawers and placed a letter on top, wet but still legible.

Back to the side of his angel's bed and leaning over he placed the lightest of kisses on her forehead. She gurgled like a baby, slowly pulling the covers closer to her neck.

Greg left her to sleep.

He closed the bathroom door. Locked it. He began to run the bath. Hot scalding water sped out of the tap. A giant gold-rimmed mirror was centred above the sink. His partner screamed and shouted obscenities at him but Greg was unfazed by this. He stopped the bath just short of overflowing and found the blades in the little cabinet under the sink.

He took a blade. Standing in front of the mirror naked and shaking with fear, he placed it against his left wrist and slashed from left to right, blood and relief spurted and poured from his body, his face draining whiter and whiter and whiter.

He took the bloody blade in his left hand as best he could. He had cut so deep with his first slash that he had severed tendons. Fumbling he raked the blade across his right wrist. Crimson blood flowed to the floor. Stumbling into the bath he sank down, slowly fading away.

Clear liquid turned to red and the snow just came down and down and down.

The Kiss

Amy McTigue
17 yrs, Tullamore Writing Group

THE CANDYFLOSS CLOUDS on the horizon fled from the dark creature that spread its cape over the land. The trees quivered in the breeze. The moon vainly gazed at its reflection in the lake, using the water as a looking glass. Just like the figure that waited on the bank. In the Moonshine the figure peered into the lake, watching curiously as the rippling water distorted her sharp features. The point of her nose softened and her cold blue eyes adopted a merry glint in the shimmering mirror.

Is this what I could be? She thought, growing impatient with her friendly reflection. Hissing to herself she waved a pale, spindly hand over the water. A mysterious mist gathered and settled on the glassy lake swirling slowly. The moon vanished behind a cloud and left the woman to wait. Moments passed, moments that seemed like an eternity. The woman's thoughts twisted around her in a dark vortex and he was the only colour she could find. Her heart fluttered.

She could feel him coming closer.

Her breath trapped in her chest. She couldn't move. He stalked closer. Butterflies rose in her stomach. Closer. The butterflies raged. She couldn't take this anymore. She despised how vulnerable he made her feel.

"Good evening," he whispered into her ear. She smiled despite herself, hating his power. The moon peeped from behind a cloud reaching out to Alexander with silver rays. His light blue hair fell casually over his right eye. Contrasting with the black mask that covered the top of his face. Revealing only his startlingly beautiful faded grey eyes.

"You shouldn't sneak up on a lady..." Her tone dropped from spring evening to frozen winter as she began mentally building a wall of icy cold bricks between him and her. Shielding herself.

"I shouldn't... I didn't frighten you... did I?" He replied. A playful smile danced across his lips and his eyes twinkled.

"The only thing that frightens me is your mask and what your hiding under it," she retorted. Alexander laughed softly. The wall she had carefully constructed was starting to crumble.

"I couldn't hide anything from you. Even if I tried..." he stepped closer.

The wall began to topple.

Alexander took another step forward, through the remains of Sapphire's broken wall, conjuring up a singe rose from beneath the folds of his long black cloak. He held the rose out. Its soft black petals blended into the night. Sapphire's pale fingers touched the rose. They stood motionless holding the rose between them, looking at each other. Alexander felt the cold creep under his fingertips. He glanced down at the bright flower. Its petals materialised in the darkness. The moon shone on its now silvery exterior. He looked up at Sapphire. Her face tilted downwards, looking at the rose between them. Watching delightfully, almost cruelly, a look of satisfaction on her face as the rose was caged in a metal prison. She looked up at him, but the cruel face she'd worn just moments before dissolved into sheer beauty again. He reached out to touch her face. Smiling sadly, he stroked the air around it but never touched it.

Can I do this to him? Sapphire wondered. Can I do this is myself? She was unwilling to answer. But the questions hung in the humid air around her. Alexander looked as if he was about to say something. He never got a chance to say it. Sapphire leaned forward and kissed him. His eyes widened in shock and then closed as he embraced her. Holding her tight. The first and last time he'd ever hold her. He wanted it to last for eternity. As they kissed, Alexander could feel silver crawling up his throat. His eyes widened. The cold metal tingled through his body. Consuming him. Sapphire pulled away from his grip. Watching him sadly as he struggled against the inevitable.

"That's why mortals should never fall in love with gods…" she said quietly as she disappeared, swirling into the lake mist.

An Roinn Gnóthaí Pobail, Tuaithe agus Gaeltachta
Department of Community, Rural and Gaeltacht Affairs

An Roinn Gnóthaí Pobail, Tuaithe agus Gaeltachta
Department of Community, Rural and Gaeltacht Affairs

An Roinn Gnóthaí Pobail, Tuaithe agus Gaeltachta
Department of Community, Rural and Gaeltacht Affairs

An Roinn Gnóthaí Pobail, Tuaithe agus Gaeltachta
Department of Community, Rural and Gaeltacht Affairs

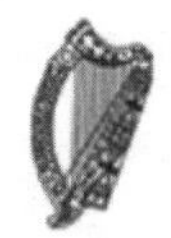

An Roinn Gnóthaí Pobail, Tuaithe agus Gaeltachta

Department of Community, Rural and Gaeltacht Affairs

An Roinn Gnóthaí Pobail, Tuaithe agus Gaeltachta
Department of Community, Rural and Gaeltacht Affairs

An Roinn Gnóthaí Pobail, Tuaithe agus Gaeltachta
Department of Community, Rural and Gaeltacht Affairs